I0778057

Constance Santego

Guardian of the Lake

Dr. Constance Santego weaves stories of love, mystery, and personal transformation set against the captivating backdrop of British Columbia's Okanagan Valley. Inspired by the natural beauty and rich legends of her surroundings, Constance crafts compelling narratives that delve into the mysteries of the human spirit and the world around us. Living in the heart of the Okanagan, she shares a fulfilling life with her husband and channels her passions for storytelling and healing into tales that resonate with readers long after the final page.

www.constancesantego.ca

Guardian of the Lake
Copyright © 2025 by Dr. Constance Santego.
All rights reserved. No part of this publication may be reproduced, distributed or transmitted in any form or by any means, including photocopying, recording, or other electronic or mechanical methods, without the prior written permission of the publisher, except in the case of brief quotations embodied in critical reviews and certain other non-commercial uses permitted by copyright law. For permission requests, write to the publisher, addressed "Attention: Permissions Coordinator," at the address below.

Published by
   Editor & Interior Layout: Dr. Constance Santego
   Book Layout: ©2017 BookDesignTemplates.com
   Soft Cover ISBN: 978-1-990062-61-2
   eBook ISBN: 978-1-990062-62-9

Created and published in Canada. Printed and bound in the United States of America
Ordering Information: csantego@gmail.com

Guardian of the Lake v

ALSO BY DR. CONSTANCE SANTEGO
NOVELS
Illegitimate Grace

Okanagan Trilogy:
Beneath the Vineyards
Under the Okanagan Sun

The Nine Spiritual Gifts Series:
Journey of a Soul – (Vol 1 Michael)
Language of a Soul – (Vol 2 Gabriel)
Prophecy of a Soul – (Vol 3 Bath Kol)
Healing of a Soul – (Vol 4 Raphael)
Miracles of a Soul – (Vol 5 Hamied)
Knowledge of a Soul – (Vol 6 Raziel)
Wisdom of a Soul – (Vol 7 Uriel)
Faith of a Soul – (Vol 8 Pistis Sophia)

NONFICTION
The Intuitive Life, The Gift Of Prophecy, Third
Edition
Fairy Tales, Dreams And Reality… Where Are You On
Your Path? Second Edition
Your Persona… The Mask You Wear
Archangel Michael's Soul Retrieval Guide
Tesla And The Future Of Energy Medicine
Beyond Tesla: *Advancing The Science Of Energy Healing*
Tesla's Code: *Mastering Energy, Frequency, And Creative
Power*
Scaling Beyond 6 Figures: *Strategies for Health & Wellness
Professionals*
Beyond the Mind: *Harnessing the Power of Astral Projection
for Creative Awakening*
Bend, Don't Break: *Finding Your Way Back to Abundance*
Ring Therapy: *A Guide to Healing and Balance*
Ring Therapy Pocket Guide

Floraopathy™: *The Art and Science of Vibrational Healing with Essential Oils*

REIKI WISDOM, SERIES:
Angelic Lifestyle, a Vibrant Lifestyle
Angelic Lifestyle 42-Day Energy Cleanse
Reiki and the Power of The Joint Points: *Unlocking Energy Pathways for Healing* (Vol I)

SECRETS OF A HEALER, SERIES:
Magic Of Aromatherapy (Vol I)
Magic Of Reflexology (Vol II)
Magic Of The Gifts (Vol III)
Magic Of Muscle Testing (Vol IV)
Magic Of Iridology (Vol V)
Magic Of Massage (Vol VI)
Magic Of Hypnotherapy (Vol VII)
Magic Of Reiki (Vol VIII)
Magic Of Advanced Aromatherapy (Vol IX)
Magic Of Esthetics (Vol X)
The Reiki Master's Manual (Vol XI)

ADULT COLORING JOURNALS
SERIES-ZEN COLORING:
Quantum Energy and Mindful Living Journal (Vol 1)
Reiki Energy Journal (Vol 2)
Nine Spiritual Gifts Journal (Vol 3)
I Forgive Journal (Vol 4)

FOR CHILDREN
I am Big Tonight. I Don't Need the Light

Dedicated

To the land of the Okanagan and its people—past, present, and future. Your beauty, resilience, and stories inspire this journey. This book is a tribute to the enduring connection between the heart, the land, and the legacy we leave behind.

Guardian of the Lake

Dr. Eleanor "Ellie" Marston: A Story of Mystery and Discovery

In the heart of the Okanagan Valley, Dr. Eleanor "Ellie" Marston arrives with a singular purpose: to uncover the truth behind the legendary Ogopogo. A marine biologist driven by a fascination with global lake legends, Ellie embarks on a journey to validate claims of underwater tunnels linking Ogopogo to other cryptids like the Loch Ness Monster.

Ellie's journey unfolds as she immerses herself in the vibrant landscapes of Okanagan Lake, navigating its shimmering depths and the rich cultural lore that surrounds it. Amid her research, she encounters Ryan Stokes, a local Syilx native artist and storyteller whose vivid depictions of the Ogopogo legend challenge her scientific perspectives. Ryan's deep connection to his heritage and commitment to preserving the lake's spiritual balance stirs something unexpected in Ellie, forcing her to confront her own biases.

As Ellie delves deeper into her investigation, strange occurrences on the lake—lights beneath the surface, inexplicable currents, and mysterious carvings—blur the line between myth and reality. Her bond with Ryan grows as they navigate the tension between scientific discovery and cultural preservation, finding in each other a shared respect for the mysteries of the natural world.

This is a story of exploration—of nature, culture, and self—set against the breathtaking backdrop of Okanagan Lake. A tribute to the courage it takes to seek the unknown and the timeless connections that bind humanity to the land, Ellie's journey is a reminder that truth often lies at the intersection of science and spirit.

The roots of our past anchor us,

but it is in exploring their mysteries—
honoring their stories and embracing
their lessons—that we find the courage
to uncover truths, grow, and chart our
course into the unknown.

Dr. Constance Santego

Fact and Disclaimer:

This novel draws upon the rich beauty and cultural heritage of the Okanagan Valley to create a fictional narrative of love, healing, and personal discovery. While real locations and elements of the region's traditions are featured, all characters, events, and specific scenarios are entirely the product of the author's imagination.

The story aims to offer readers a heartfelt exploration of the human spirit, set against the stunning backdrop of Kelowna's vineyards, lakes, and vibrant community. It reflects themes of resilience, connection, and the courage to embrace life's unexpected turns.

Any resemblance to actual persons, living or deceased, or real events is purely coincidental.

Prologue

The waters of Okanagan Lake shimmered under the pale moonlight, stretching into the darkness like a mirror to the heavens. A soft breeze rustled the pines along the shore, carrying with it the scent of summer and the whispers of stories long forgotten. Beneath the surface, the lake seemed alive, its depths holding secrets that time itself had refused to relinquish.

For centuries, the Syilx people had called this place sacred, a cradle of life and mystery. They spoke of a guardian, a creature not bound by flesh and blood alone but by spirit—Ogopogo, the keeper of balance, the watcher of the waters. To some, it was a legend, a tale spun to enchant and warn. To others, it was as real as the lake itself.

In recent years, the legend has become fodder for tabloids and tourists, reducing its essence to a caricature. But those who listened closely to the whispers of the valley knew better. The lake's stillness was not emptiness. It was a silence that spoke volumes.

On this night, the silence was broken. A ripple formed in the moonlit expanse, followed by another and another until the stillness was replaced by a gentle surge. To the untrained eye, it could have been the wind, a passing school of fish, or a trick of the light. But those who knew the lake's rhythms would have felt it—an awakening.

Far from the shore, a shadow moved beneath the surface, vast and serpentine, a fleeting presence that seemed to watch as much as it was watched. Then, as quickly as it had come, it was gone, leaving the lake to its reflections and the night to its mysteries.

The stories of Ogopogo had always been about more than a creature. They were about the connection between people and the land, the balance of nature, and the respect it commanded. But now, as the world encroached further into the valley, the question lingered, could balance be preserved, or would the guardian rise to remind them of what was at stake?

Chapter 1

The lake was eerily quiet, its surface a vast mirror reflecting the scattered lights of nearby cabins. The air carried a cool bite, a reminder that even summer nights in the Okanagan could hold a chill. Jack Armitage, a middle-aged tourist from Lethbridge, Alberta, leaned against the railing of the rental pontoon boat, his hands trembling slightly as he clutched a thermos of coffee. The lake had drawn him in, promising solace and an escape from his recent divorce. But tonight, the stillness felt oppressive.

The faint hum of the boat's motor broke the silence as it drifted closer to Rattlesnake Island, a place Jack had read about in brochures filled with tales of the legendary Ogopogo. He had laughed it off, dismissing the stories as local folklore. Now, he wasn't so sure.

The water beneath the boat seemed to ripple unnaturally, though there was no breeze. Jack leaned over the edge, his breath catching as he spotted a shadow moving just below the surface. It was massive—far too large to be a fish. He stumbled back, his thermos clattering to the deck, spilling coffee laced with whiskey across the pristine white surface.

A sudden, violent jolt rocked the boat. Jack barely managed to grab hold of the railing as the vessel tipped dangerously to one side. Heart pounding, he scrambled to the control panel and tried to steer away from the island, but the motor sputtered and died. The boat drifted aimlessly, the silence now broken only by the sound of his ragged breathing.

Then he saw it. A serpentine shape, illuminated faintly by the moonlight, broke the surface briefly before disappearing again into the depths. Jack fumbled for his phone, his hands shaking as he tried to capture a picture, but the screen only showed darkness. He cursed under his breath and dialed emergency services, his voice cracking as he shouted into the phone.

"Something's out here! Something huge! My boat—it's not moving!"

By the time the rescue team arrived, Jack was visibly shaken, his eyes wide with fear. "I swear," he told the responders, "I saw it. The Ogopogo. It's real."

The following morning, the Okanagan buzzed with news of the incident. Headlines splashed across social media and local news outlets proclaimed: Tourist Claims Ogopogo Attack on Okanagan Lake.

Dr. Ellie Marston scrolled through the article on her phone, her breakfast untouched. A marine biologist with a penchant for debunking myths, Ellie had spent years chasing freshwater anomalies, from North America's Great Lakes to Scotland's Loch Ness. The Ogopogo was next on her list, and this story was the perfect excuse to make the trip.

She pulled up her calendar and cleared her schedule. "Time to see what's really going on," she muttered to herself, a mix of skepticism and excitement flickering in her hazel eyes.

Meanwhile, Claire Bennett sat in Ethan's kitchen, sipping tea and staring at the same headline. The burnout she had been battling for months lifted slightly as curiosity sparked within her. A seasoned travel writer, Claire had covered everything from bustling metropolises to secluded beaches, but this— this was different. The lake she now called home held a story she couldn't resist.

Her phone buzzed. It was Emily Fraser, her friend and now a celebrated photographer.

"Did you see the news?" Emily asked, her voice tinged with excitement.

"Of course," Claire replied. "What do you make of it?"

"Funny you ask," Emily said. "I was out snapping photos on the lake last night. I didn't see anything, but when I reviewed my shots this morning… there's something there. Something I can't explain."

Claire's heart skipped a beat. "Send it to me."

Within moments, an image appeared on her screen. The photo was haunting, a faint, elongated shape beneath the water's surface, framed by moonlit ripples. It could have been a trick of the light, but it was enough to send a shiver down Claire's spine.

"We need to follow this up," Claire said firmly. "I'll meet you at your cabin later this afternoon."

Emily hesitated. "Do you really think it could be…?"

Claire didn't answer right away. Instead, she stared at the photo, a mix of awe and apprehension filling her chest.

"Let's find out."

Chapter 2

The Kelowna Capital Newspaper has been a cornerstone of the community since its founding in 1920, chronicling the valley's history through world wars, economic shifts, and the ebb and flow of its ever-growing population. Once a humble weekly publication, it had evolved into a trusted daily news source, celebrated for its commitment to preserving the stories of the Okanagan Valley while embracing modern journalism. For Emily Fraser and Claire Bennett, working at the newspaper wasn't just a job. It was a way to connect with their new home and amplify the voices of its people.

Emily adjusted her camera lens, her fingers deftly working the controls as she captured the early morning light glinting off Okanagan

Lake. She had always loved how the golden hues danced across the water—a photographer's dream and a hallmark of the valley's beauty.

"How's it going?" Claire's voice interrupted Emily's focus. She turned to see her friend, notepad in hand, her hair pulled back into a loose ponytail. Claire's determined expression hinted at her relentless pursuit of the truth, a trait that made her one of the Capital's most respected reporters.

"The light's perfect," Emily replied, glancing at the shots on her camera. "And this lake… it never disappoints. But honestly, the real story isn't the scenery. It's that tourist's encounter last night."

Claire nodded. "The Ogopogo sighting? The editors are already buzzing. They want a feature for tomorrow's edition. Looks like we're working together on this one."

Emily grinned. "It's about time. I'll handle the visuals. You handle the words."

Inside the newspaper's office—a modernized building that still bore traces of its original architecture—Claire and Emily set up their workspace. The open-plan office buzzed with the sounds of ringing phones, clacking keyboards, and the occasional burst of laughter or debate. The walls were adorned with historic front pages, including the paper's earliest editions reporting on the construction of the Kettle Valley Railway and the region's booming orchard industry.

Claire stared at the blank page on her screen, her mind racing with angles to approach the story. She knew the Ogopogo was more than just a legend. It was a symbol of the valley's identity, woven into the fabric of its culture and economy. Tourism brochures flaunted its image, local artists celebrated it in their work, and children grew up with tales of the lake's mysterious guardian.

"Hey," Emily said, sliding her camera onto the desk. "Check this out." She pulled up an image on her laptop, the same haunting shot she had shown Claire the day before. "I tried enhancing the contrast. Look at the shape beneath the water."

Claire leaned in, her breath catching as she examined the photo. The elongated shadow seemed almost serpentine, its outline faint but unmistakable.

"This could be the real deal," Claire said, her voice tinged with awe. "Or at least enough to get people talking."

"That's the plan," Emily replied. "We've got the perfect combo—facts and visuals. Let's give the people a story they'll remember."

As the day wore on, Claire pieced together a narrative that balanced the eyewitness account of the tourist with the scientific skepticism of local experts. She even reached out to Dr. Ellie Marston, who she had just heard was heading to Kelowna, for a quote.

"The Ogopogo is fascinating, but let's not jump to conclusions," Ellie told her over the phone. "What you're describing could be explained by natural phenomena. That said, I'm looking forward to exploring the lake myself."

Claire included the quote, knowing it would lend credibility to the article while keeping the mystery alive. Meanwhile, Emily selected her most evocative photographs, from the shadowy figure beneath the water to atmospheric shots of the lake at dawn.

By evening, the article and accompanying photos were ready to go to press. The headline read: *"Shadows in the Depths: Renewed Sightings Stir Ogopogo Mystery."*

As the first copies rolled off the press, Claire and Emily stood together in the newsroom, holding the freshly printed paper.

"Here's to another story," Claire said, raising her coffee cup in a mock toast.

"And to the mysteries that keep us coming back," Emily added, her camera slung over her shoulder.

Chapter 3

The drive across Okanagan Lake was calm, the water stretching out like a sheet of polished silver beneath the morning sun. Dr. Eleanor "Ellie" Marston gripped the steering wheel, her auburn hair swept into a loose braid, with the car windows cracked just enough to let in the light breeze. Her hazel eyes, sharp and inquisitive, flicked between the road ahead and the shimmering lake that seemed to stretch endlessly alongside her. As Kelowna came into view, the vibrant hillsides dotted with vineyards and orchards framed the town like a postcard, stirring a mix of anticipation and curiosity within her.

Ellie had a presence that commanded attention—not in an overtly assertive way, but in how she carried herself. At just over five and a half feet tall, her petite frame was balanced by an air of quiet confidence. Her well-worn leather satchel, slung across one shoulder, contained notebooks, field guides, and a small laptop—a working professional's survival kit. Dressed in a casual yet practical outfit of olive-green cargo pants and a chambray shirt rolled up to her elbows, she looked every bit the scientist she was.

Originally from the Lower Mainland of British Columbia, Ellie's fascination with aquatic ecosystems began during childhood summers spent at her grandparents' cabin in Harrison Hot Springs. Her grandfather had been a fisherman. His tales of the elusive *Sturgeon of Harrison Lake* ignited a lifelong curiosity in her. Unlike her peers, who outgrew stories of mythical creatures, Ellie had turned her fascination into a career— albeit one grounded in science.

Her academic and professional achievements have made her a prominent figure in the field of marine biology. She earned her doctorate at the University of British Columbia, and her dissertation focused on the behavioral patterns of bioluminescent plankton in temperate lakes. From there, she went on to work with leading research teams, studying everything from the invasive Asian carp in North America's Great Lakes to rare freshwater dolphins in the Amazon.

But what had truly cemented Ellie's reputation was her work in Scotland, where she had been part of a project investigating the infamous Loch Ness. Her findings, while not uncovering Nessie herself, had revealed new species of micro-organisms unique to the loch's ecosystem—an achievement that landed her a feature in National Geographic.

Now in her early forties, Ellie had developed a healthy skepticism when it came to legends. "Every myth," she often said, "Has a kernel of truth. The fun lies in separating the two." Yet the Ogopogo intrigued her. Unlike other lake monsters, the Syilx First Nation's stories gave the creature cultural significance, describing it as a protector of the land rather than a menace.

Her arrival in Kelowna wasn't just about chasing headlines. It was a chance to explore the intersection of myth and science in a region renowned for its natural beauty. She had already arranged to meet with local historians and biologists, eager to gather perspectives before heading out onto the lake herself.

As Ellie pulled into the parking lot of the modest bed-and-breakfast she had booked for the week, she paused to take in her surroundings. The warm Okanagan sun painted the landscape in shades of gold and green, with the vineyards on the hillsides creating a patchwork quilt of lush growth. She stepped out of the car, her leather satchel slung over one shoulder, and took a deep breath, the scent of pine and distant water mingling in the air.

The innkeeper greeted her warmly as she entered the charming lodge overlooking the lake. Handing her a key, he gave her a knowing smile. "You're here for the Ogopogo, aren't you?"

Ellie chuckled softly, setting her bag down by her feet. "Isn't everyone?"

She dropped her bags in her room and immediately set up a temporary workspace. Maps of the lake were spread across the desk, annotated with potential research sites. A whiteboard leaned against the wall, already scribbled with questions and hypotheses.

Her first step would be to meet with the tourist from the previous night's sighting, Jack Armitage. Though she doubted his story was more than exaggerated panic, she knew better than to dismiss eyewitness accounts entirely. In her experience, people often saw *something*—a disturbance in the water, an unusual shape, a flicker of movement—but the human mind had a way of filling in blanks with imagination.

Ellie's phone buzzed, interrupting her thoughts. It was Claire Bennett, the journalist who had reached out for a quote the previous day.

"I'm glad you took my call," Claire said after pleasantries were exchanged. "Would you be willing to collaborate on the investigation? Your expertise would be invaluable."

Ellie hesitated. "I usually work independently. But this story is too intriguing to pass up. Let's meet tomorrow and discuss how to move forward."

After hanging up, Ellie returned to her notes, her mind alight with possibilities. She jotted down a reminder to connect with the Syilx Nation's cultural liaison. Understanding the stories passed down through generations would be just as critical as analyzing water samples.

Before turning in for the night, she stood at the window, gazing out at the lake. It stretched endlessly, shimmering under the moonlight. Somewhere out there, a mystery awaited her. Whether it was a new species, an optical illusion, or the remnants of an ancient legend, Ellie was determined to uncover the truth.

Chapter 4

The early afternoon sun cast a golden hue over the Rotary Centre for the Arts, its contemporary architecture blending seamlessly with the surrounding natural landscape. Dr. Ellie parked her car on the street and stepped out, her satchel in tow. She had been grappling with Claire and Emily's offer to collaborate, but something about teaming up with reporters felt too sensationalist for her methodical approach. For now, she wanted to go straight to the source—the people who had been telling stories of the Ogopogo long before tourists ever flocked to the lake.

Inside the center, a series of vibrant paintings adorned the walls, each one depicting the Okanagan Valley through the eyes of the Syilx people. Ellie's gaze lingered on a striking canvas near the entrance of the exhibit, a serpentine figure, its body coiled in graceful arcs, emerging from the shimmering waters of the lake, titled The Ogopogo.

"Beautiful, isn't it?" a voice said from behind her.

Ellie turned to see a man in his early thirties with an athletic build and long dark hair tied back in a low ponytail. His deep-set dark brown eyes radiated warmth, though they held an intensity that made Ellie instantly curious. He wore a well-worn denim jacket over a T-shirt bearing an intricate design of the Ogopogo, his hands stained with flecks of paint.

"Ryan Stokes," he introduced himself, extending a hand.

Ellie shook it. "Dr. Eleanor Marston. You're the artist behind these?"

Ryan nodded, gesturing toward the paintings. "Guilty as charged. But I don't just paint—I tell the stories, too."

"That's actually why I'm here," Ellie said, her tone shifting to one of professional curiosity. "I've read about the Ogopogo for years, but I'd like to hear the stories directly from someone who knows their origins. The Syilx perspective."

Ryan's expression softened, and he motioned for her to follow him into a smaller adjoining gallery. The room was quieter, its walls adorned with more of his work. A large mural dominated one side, depicting a swirling underwater scene with the Ogopogo at its center. Around the mural, smaller illustrations told a visual story, showing the creature interacting with its surroundings—protecting, warning, and guiding.

"To the Syilx people," Ryan began, "The Ogopogo isn't just some monster. It's a spirit, a guardian of the water and the land. The stories have been passed down for generations, long before the settlers arrived and turned it into a tourist attraction."

Ellie's brow furrowed as she studied the mural. "A guardian? Most of what I've read paints it as a threat or something to be feared."

Ryan let out a short laugh. "That's because people fear what they don't understand. The Ogopogo isn't a predator; it's a reminder—to respect the land, the water, and everything they provide. The legend warns against greed and taking more than you need."

Ellie nodded thoughtfully. "And the sightings? What are the accounts from tourists and locals over the years? How do you see those fitting into the legend?"

Ryan tilted his head, considering her question. "Some might be real, some might be wishful thinking. But the truth doesn't matter as much as what the stories teach us. That's the beauty of oral traditions—they're alive and evolving. The Ogopogo might not look the same to every generation, but the message stays the same."

Ellie couldn't help but feel drawn to his perspective. As a scientist, she was accustomed to seeking empirical evidence, yet there was something compelling about the idea of legends serving as living metaphors.

"Would you be willing to share more of these stories with me?" Ellie asked. "I'm not just here to debunk myths—I want to understand the cultural significance behind them."

Ryan regarded her for a moment as if weighing her sincerity. Finally, he nodded. "Come by my studio tomorrow. I'll show you more of my work, and we'll talk."

"Thank you," Ellie said earnestly.

Chapter 5

The sun was just beginning to dip below the horizon as Ellie's car crossed the Kelowna bridge, heading west. The lake shimmered in the golden light, its vastness calming and mysterious at once. She followed Highway 97 to Westbank, her GPS leading her to a modest building tucked into a cluster of trees. Ryan's studio sat on Indian land, its exterior a mix of natural wood and modern glass, blending harmoniously with the surrounding environment.

Ellie stepped out of her car, her satchel in hand, and took in the quiet beauty of the area. She was about to knock on the studio door when she heard voices inside. Pushing it open, she found Ryan speaking with two women standing in the center of the room, their faces lighting up as they saw her.

"You must be Ellie!" Claire said with a grin. "Fancy meeting you here."

Ellie raised an eyebrow. "Who are you?"

"I spoke with you earlier, Claire Bennett, and this is Emily Fraser."

Emily held up her camera. "Ryan invited us to capture some of his work for a feature we're putting together."

Ellie sighed, glancing at Ryan, who stood near a workbench at the back of the studio, organizing brushes and paints.

Claire's grin widened. "See? Even the universe thinks we should team up. It must be fate."

Ryan cleared his throat, stepping forward. "Well, since you're all here, I suppose it's a good time to share one of the stories." He gestured to a small circle of chairs near the mural he had painted, a sprawling depiction of the Ogopogo woven into the natural beauty of the Okanagan Valley.

The three women settled into their seats as Ryan took his place in front of them. He began with a pause as though inviting the weight of the story to settle into the room.

"The Syilx call the Ogopogo, nx̌ax̌aitkʷ," Ryan said, his voice low and steady. "It means 'Sacred Spirit of the Lake.' The stories go back long before any of us, passed down from elders who walked these lands when the valley was untouched by modern life."

Ellie leaned forward, her curiosity piqued.

"There's one story," Ryan continued, "About a time when the nx̌ax̌aitkʷ appeared to the people as a warning. It was many generations ago, during a long, dry summer. The waters of the lake were lower than anyone could remember, and the people were struggling to catch enough fish to feed their families. In desperation, some of the younger hunters set out at night, ignoring the elders' advice to leave an offering for the spirit before fishing.

"That night, as their canoe glided across the still waters near Rattlesnake Island, they saw something rise from the depths. It was massive, its body shimmering like the scales of a great serpent, but its eyes—they weren't the eyes of a predator. They were ancient, knowing, filled with both sorrow and power.

"The young men panicked, trying to flee, but the canoe was struck by a sudden wave, tipping them into the water. They struggled to shore, shaken but unharmed, and the spirit disappeared. The next morning, the elders found the hunters and told them the truth, the nx̌ax̌aitkʷ wasn't punishing them—it was warning them. The lake's balance had been disturbed, and if they didn't change their ways, there would be consequences.

"The people heeded the warning, restoring the lake's harmony by honoring its gifts and taking only what they needed. Over time, the waters rose again, and the fish returned."

As Ryan finished, the room was silent. The weight of the story lingered in the air, a mixture of reverence and reflection.

"So, you are saying that it's not just a monster," Ellie said softly, her voice breaking the quiet. "But a guardian."

Ryan nodded. "Exactly. The nx̌ax̌aitkʷ isn't something to fear—it's something to respect. It represents balance, a connection to the land and water that sustains us. That's why we tell these stories—to remind people of what really matters."

Emily glanced at Claire, then back at Ellie. "I think this is something we all need to tell together."

Ellie hesitated, her scientific mind still wary of sensationalism, but she couldn't deny the power of the story she had just heard. Perhaps Claire was right—perhaps fate really had brought them together.

"Meet us tomorrow at 10 a.m. at Bliss Bakery on Ellis Street," Claire said to Ellie with a warm smile.

Chapter 6

The next morning, Ellie parked her car on Ellis Street, the scent of freshly baked pastries wafting through the air as she approached Bliss Bakery. The quaint café was already bustling, its cozy interior filled with the hum of conversation and the soft clink of ceramic cups.

Inside, Claire and Emily were seated at a small corner table, a half-eaten croissant and a steaming cup of tea in front of Claire. She waved Ellie over with an eager smile.

"Ellie! Over here!"

Ellie slid into the seat across from them, setting her satchel down beside her. Before she could even glance at the menu, Claire leaned forward, her voice brimming with enthusiasm.

"You *have* to try the Chai Tiger Spice tea latte," Claire said, her eyes sparkling. "It's to die for. Seriously, it's like a warm hug in a cup."

Ellie raised an eyebrow, smirking. "Well, with that kind of endorsement, how can I say no?"

She went to the counter and ordered the latte along with a cranberry scone. Moments later, the drink arrived, its spiced aroma rising in a cloud of steam. Ellie took a cautious sip and was pleasantly surprised by the perfect balance of sweetness and spice.

"Okay," Ellie admitted, setting the cup down. "You weren't exaggerating. This is amazing."

"Told you," Claire said with a grin. "And if you're a coffee drinker, you've got to try Cherry Hill Coffee sometime. They've been hand-roasting organic beans right here in Kelowna since 1986. Their blends are exceptional—a true taste of the Okanagan."

Emily, camera slung over her chair, leaned in. "Alright, now that we've got the important stuff out of the way, let's talk about the Ogopogo," Ellie said, taking another sip of her latte.

"Well," Claire began, "There's been a fair share of documentaries on the subject. Have you seen any of them?"

Ellie nodded. "A few. Most of them seem to focus on shaky video footage or grainy photographs, making it easy to dismiss the whole thing as a hoax."

"That's true," Emily agreed. "But there was one I watched years ago that took a different angle. It delved into the Syilx stories and the cultural significance of the Ogopogo. It wasn't just about proving or disproving its existence—it was about understanding what it represents."

"That's the approach I respect," Ellie said. "I've seen too many documentaries treat it like a sideshow attraction."

Claire tapped her mug thoughtfully. "There was one I remember from the early 2000s—*Mysteries of the Deep*, I think it was called. It included interviews with locals and Syilx elders, but it also had that dramatic music and ominous narration that made it feel a bit like a horror movie."

Ellie laughed. "I think I've seen that one. The narrator kept saying, 'Could it be... the Ogopogo?' in that overly dramatic tone."

Emily joined in the laughter. "Exactly! But it did have some interesting segments about geological formations in the lake and how they could create unusual currents or shadows."

Claire nodded. "True, but I feel like those kinds of explanations always miss the point. Whether it's real or not, the Ogopogo is part of this place's identity. It's woven into the culture and the history."

Emily leaned forward, her excitement evident. "Did you know Leonard Nimoy hosted an episode about the Ogopogo on his show *In Search of...* back in the 1970s? It's such a classic, and he really dives into the cultural and scientific perspectives."

Claire shook her head no.

"That's why I'm here," Ellie said, her tone more serious now. "I want to explore that intersection of science and storytelling. Maybe there's a way to bring both perspectives together in a way that respects the legend without sensationalizing it."

Emily leaned back, her expression thoughtful. "Sounds like we've got some digging to do. Between Ryan's stories, the Syilx traditions, and the scientific mysteries of the lake, there's more than enough for a compelling project."

Claire raised her cup in a mock toast. "To uncovering the truth—whatever it might be."

Ellie clinked her mug against Claire's, a smile tugging at her lips. "To balance," she said. "Between legend and fact."

Chapter 7

The next day, the warm hum of conversation filled Bliss Bakery as Ellie walked in, spotting Claire and Emily already seated at the table near the window. Claire had her laptop open, a notebook sprawled beside it, while Emily fiddled with her camera, scrolling through photos she had taken the day before.

"Morning," Ellie greeted as she slid into her seat, setting her satchel down. She placed an order for another Chai Tiger Spice tea latte, now her new favorite thanks to Claire.

"Morning!" Claire said, her voice tinged with excitement. "We've been digging into all kinds of Ogopogo-related material since yesterday, and there's a lot to unpack."

Emily nodded, glancing up from her camera. "I've got some older footage of the lake that we could analyze later. But first, we wanted to go over everything we've learned so far and see how it all fits together."

Ellie sipped her latte as Claire opened a document on her laptop, listing various notes they'd compiled.

Claire started. "So, from Ryan, we know that the Syilx call the Ogopogo nx̌ax̌aitkʷ, the 'Sacred Spirit of the Lake.' He believes it is a guardian, not a monster. The legend is less about danger and more about balance— protecting the land, the water, and their resources. It's a warning against greed and disrespecting nature."

Ellie nodded thoughtfully. "That perspective shifts everything. It's not just about finding a creature but understanding what it represents culturally."

Emily took over. "Then we have the modern sightings. People have described a long, serpentine creature breaking the surface of the water. Some of these accounts go back decades—like Art Folden's video in the 1960s or Ken Chaplin's footage in 1989."

Claire added, "Though some of those were debunked. Remember that case where it turned out to be a beaver? And the one where it was just unusual wave patterns caused by the wind?"

Ellie smirked. "Those don't surprise me. People want to believe, and the brain has a way of filling in gaps. But still, the consistency of these descriptions across decades is intriguing."

Claire pointed to a bullet point in her notes. "From the documentaries we reviewed, there are some interesting theories. MonsterQuest talked about underwater caves that could support a large creature, while Is It Real? Suggested unusual currents and geological phenomena could explain sightings. And then there's the idea that the Ogopogo could be a surviving species of prehistoric marine reptile."

Ellie raised an eyebrow. "That last one's a stretch, but the geological aspects are worth exploring. If there are underwater caves, they could be creating conditions that mimic movement—shadows, currents, even strange waves."

Emily gestured to her camera. "We can't ignore how much of this is fueled by media and tourism. The Ogopogo isn't just a legend—it's a symbol of the Okanagan. It's on signs, sculptures, even children's books. The stories might be old, but the modern narrative keeps evolving to draw people in."

Claire nodded. "Right. And that's where the truth gets murky. How much of what people claim to see is influenced by the idea of the Ogopogo as a tourist attraction? Are they seeing the creature, or are they seeing what they want to see?"

Ellie leaned forward, adding her perspective. "One thing we haven't talked about much yet is the lake itself. It's deep—nearly 800 feet in some places. The sheer size and depth make it perfect for hiding things, whether it's geological phenomena or something alive. The water is also glacial, which could explain why it preserves unusual organic material or creates strange optical illusions."

Claire tapped her pen against her notebook. "So, we've got culture, eyewitness accounts, science, and media all swirling around the same central question: What is the Ogopogo, and what does it mean to this place?"

Emily grinned. "I think we need to get out there ourselves. Boat trip, anyone?"

Ellie chuckled. "Let's not jump the gun. If we're going out on the lake, we need to be prepared—equipment, contacts, maybe even some help from Ryan for the cultural angle."

Claire leaned back, her expression thoughtful. "Agreed. But for now, we keep digging. Between the three of us, we're bound to uncover something new—whether it's a clue to the Ogopogo's existence or a deeper understanding of why this legend has lasted so long."

Ellie raised her latte. "To research, teamwork, and figuring out the mystery—whatever it might be."

Claire and Emily raised their cups with matching smiles. "To the Ogopogo," they said in unison, the energy at the table charged with anticipation.

Chapter 8

The rhythmic creak of wood and the faint scent of varnish filled the air inside Liam's boathouse, nestled along the lake's edge. Liam Fraser, Emily's husband, stood over an old wooden skiff, his sleeves rolled up and hands expertly sanding down the surface. The golden afternoon light spilled through the open doors, glinting off the water and casting a warm glow over the space.

Emily leaned against one of the beams, her camera dangling from her neck as she snapped a few candid shots of Liam at work.

"You're really putting some love into this one," she teased.

Liam looked up, smirking. "Every boat's got a story, Em. This one just needs a little help remembering it."

Before Emily could reply, the sound of crunching gravel outside announced the arrival of another visitor. Henry appeared in the doorway, his frame silhouetted against the light.

"Henry!" Liam called, straightening up. "What brings you by?"

Henry tipped his hat and stepped inside, his weathered face breaking into a grin. "Heard you were working on another beauty and thought I'd drop by. Besides," he added, glancing at Emily, "I owe this one a story about the Ogopogo."

Emily perked up. "Perfect timing. I was just telling Liam about all the theories we've been digging into."

Henry chuckled, settling into a chair near the workbench. "Well, let me add one more to the mix. It's about sturgeon."

"Sturgeon?" Liam echoed, wiping his hands on a rag.

Henry nodded, leaning back as he began his tale. "You've seen the lake—it's vast, deep, and cold. Perfect for sturgeon. White sturgeon, to be precise. They're ancient fish, practically living fossils, and they can grow massive—ten, maybe twelve feet long, and weigh well over a thousand pounds. And let me tell you, they're not shy about making their presence known."

Liam raised an eyebrow. "I've heard of big fish, but that sounds more like a lake monster to me."

Henry grinned. "You're not far off. Now imagine this, you've got two, maybe three of these giants swimming together, their backs breaking the surface in a steady rhythm. From a distance, it'd look just like a serpent— moving up and down, creating that undulating motion people always describe."

Emily's eyes widened. "That would explain some of the sightings. But are there really sturgeon that big in the lake?"

Henry leaned forward, his voice dropping slightly. "Oh, I've seen them. Years ago, I was fishing near Rattlesnake Island when something huge swam under my boat. It was slow, deliberate, and big enough to make me rethink every Ogopogo story I'd ever heard. And I'm not the only one. Plenty of old-timers will tell you about the sturgeon they've spotted—or the ones that got away."

Liam crossed his arms, intrigued. "But sturgeon don't usually come to the surface, do they?"

Henry shrugged. "Not often, but they do when they're feeding or spawning. And when they do, they make quite the spectacle. Now,

I'm not saying every Ogopogo sighting is sturgeon, but it sure explains a fair share of them."

Emily raised her camera, snapping a shot of Henry mid-story. "So, what you're saying is, Ogopogo might not be a single creature at all—it could be a group of sturgeon working together to keep the legend alive."

Henry chuckled. "Exactly. Sometimes, the truth is stranger—and more fascinating—than fiction."

Liam glanced at Emily, his lips curling into a smile. "Looks like you've got another piece to your puzzle."

Emily nodded thoughtfully. "And another perspective to explore. Thanks, Henry. That was… illuminating."

Henry tipped his hat again, standing up. "Always happy to share a tale or two. Just don't forget to give those sturgeon the credit they deserve."

As Henry left the boathouse, Emily turned to Liam, a glimmer of excitement in her eyes. "What do you think?"

Liam smirked, picking up his sanding block again. "I think I've got a lot of respect for sturgeon—and for storytellers like Henry.

Chapter 9

Claire was sorting through her inbox at the Kelowna Capital Newspaper when an email subject line caught her eye: "Old Ogopogo Story - Missing Bone?". She clicked, her curiosity piqued.

The message was from Bruce Hammond, a semi-retired editor who had spent over four decades chronicling the Okanagan's lesser-known tales. Claire respected his encyclopedic memory of the valley's lore and his knack for unearthing long-forgotten clippings.

Claire,

Thought you'd be interested in this. I remembered an article about a vertebra found in the 1880s. It was supposedly from a whale and pulled out of Okanagan Lake. There's a lot of mystery around it—where it came from, how it ended up in a freshwater lake, and, more importantly, how it vanished from the museum archives decades ago. Might be worth a story, especially with all this Ogopogo buzz. Check the attached notes and let me know what you think.

Claire opened the attachment, an old black-and-white photograph of a large, weathered bone and a scan of a dusty archival article from 1902. A handwritten note in the margin read, "Museum received the specimen from Vernon. No current record found."

She sat back, heart thudding. A real artifact? One tied directly to the lake? She had to share this.

That afternoon, Claire arranged to meet with Emily, Ellie, Liam, and Ethan at Liam's boathouse, a cozy space filled with the scent of cedar, engine oil, and fresh lake air. Wooden hulls in various stages of restoration lined the walls, and scattered tools gave the room a lived-in warmth.

Emily greeted Ellie first, still slightly reserved but clearly warming to the group.

Liam looked up from a sanding bench, brushing dust from his hands. Walking towards the three, "Good to see you, Claire."

Claire introduced Liam to Ellie.

"Nice to meet you," he said. "I would shake your hand, but as you can see it is quite dirty."

Ellie smiled.

Ethan leaned against the workbench, offering a quiet nod. His calm presence was grounding, especially as Claire launched into her discovery.

"I just got this from Bruce Hammond," she said, holding up a printed copy of the email and photo. "It's a vertebra that was supposedly pulled out of Okanagan Lake in the late 1800s. It's big enough to be from a whale. It was cataloged by the Vernon government agent, sent to a museum… and then vanished."

Ellie raised an eyebrow. "A whale vertebra? In a freshwater lake? That doesn't make sense biologically."

"Exactly," Claire said. "Which is why it's so strange. And if it wasn't a whale… what was it?"

Liam stepped closer, examining the grainy photograph. "I've seen a lot of bones from old logs and driftwood misidentified, but this... this looks anatomical. Vertebral. And big."

Emily, peering over Claire's shoulder, whispered, "You don't think it could be…?"

"Ogopogo?" Claire finished for her. "Or something related. Maybe not the creature itself, but a cousin? Or a long-dead relative?"

Ellie studied the image more intently now. "Or maybe it is from a whale. Maybe someone planted it. But then... why did it disappear from the museum? Why not just disprove it publicly?"

Ethan finally spoke. "Or someone didn't want it examined too closely."

The room fell into silence.

Claire looked around at the group. "We need to find out more. If there are records, maybe they're buried in the Kelowna archives or the museum's off-site storage. Bruce said there was never a follow-up article. The story just disappeared."

Liam nodded. "I can reach out to a friend at the heritage society. If that bone ever passed through their hands, he might know something."

Emily lifted her camera. "And I'll start digging through visual archives. If that bone showed up in an old display or even in the background of a photograph, I'll find it."

Ellie gave a reluctant smile. "Looks like I'm in too. I want to see if there are any biological records. Anything unusual in the lake samples over the decades."

Claire grinned, energized. "We follow the bone. We follow the mystery. Maybe it leads us to more than we expected."

Outside the boathouse, the lake shimmered in the waning light, its stillness once again hiding secrets in its depths.

Chapter 10

The next day, Claire arrived at one of her favorite spots in the Okanagan, Kelly O'Bryan's Restaurant. It was near the City Park on Bernard Avenue. Its rooftop patio overlooked the water, offering a tranquil view of the rippling surface framed by rolling hills. She arrived a little early, choosing a table under the shade of the canopy.

Moments later, Margaret walked in, her hair pinned neatly under a sunhat and her smile as warm as ever. She spotted Claire and waved before making her way over.

"Claire Bennett," Margaret greeted, pulling Claire into a quick hug. "It's been far too long! What brings you back to the valley?"

Claire smiled. "It's good to see you too, Margaret. I've missed this place—and your B&B. How's business?"

"Busy as ever," Margaret replied, settling into the chair across from Claire. "Hey, did you know that before Kelly O'Bryan's took its place as a lively Irish pub and restaurant, this building was home to Jonathan L. Seagull's, a beloved eatery that held its own charm in the heart of the Okanagan. Before its days as a restaurant, the building originally served as the home of the Royal Bank of Canada.

"No, I didn't know that," Claire replied with a smile.

"What have you been up to? Are you here on assignment?" Margaret asked, her curiosity evident.

Claire nodded, her smile turning sheepish. "Sort of. I moved here a few weeks ago. I'm actually investigating something a little… out of the ordinary. Ogopogo sightings."

Margaret's eyes lit up with curiosity. "The Ogopogo? Now, that's a topic I wasn't expecting! What's sparked your interest in the lake's legendary monster?"

Claire chuckled. "A combination of curiosity, local stories, and a few interesting eyewitness accounts. It's been fascinating so far, but there's still so much to uncover."

Margaret leaned back, her expression turning thoughtful. "You know, I might have a story for you. It's not much, but it's one of those moments I'll never forget."

Claire leaned forward, intrigued. "I'm all ears."

Margaret took a sip of her tea before beginning. "This was about thirty years ago. My husband and I were out on the lake with his brother and my sister-in-law. The guys were up at the front of the boat, taking their time and enjoying the scenery, while we ladies were sitting in the back, relaxing and chatting. It was one of those perfect summer days—calm water, clear skies, not a care in the world."

She paused a glimmer of nostalgia in her eyes. "Then, out of nowhere, my sister-in-law and I both froze. Something caught our attention in the water. It wasn't a wave or a shadow—it was moving, undulating, like a giant snake cutting through the surface."

Claire's eyes widened. "What did you do?"

"We looked at each other, completely stunned," Margaret said, shaking her head. "Neither of us could believe what we were seeing. By the time we got the guys to turn the boat around, there was nothing there—just calm water. But for those few moments… we were convinced we'd seen the Ogopogo."

"Did anyone else see it?" Claire asked.

Margaret sighed, a rueful smile on her lips. "No, just the two of us. The guys thought we were imagining things, of course. But we weren't drunk, and we weren't tired—it felt real, Claire. I'll never forget how it moved. It wasn't like anything I'd ever seen before."

Claire jotted a quick note in her journal. "That's incredible. Thank you for sharing that. It's stories like these that make the legend so compelling—so personal."

Margaret smiled. "I hope it helps. The Ogopogo might be a mystery, but it's also a part of this place. Whatever it is, it keeps the lake's magic alive."

Claire nodded, glancing out at the water shimmering in the distance. "That's what I'm starting to realize. It's not just about finding answers—it's about understanding what the Ogopogo means to people."

Margaret reached across the table, giving Claire's hand a gentle squeeze. "Good luck, dear. I can't wait to hear what you discover."

As Margaret stood to leave, Claire remained seated for a moment, her thoughts swirling. The lake held so many stories, so many secrets. And with every tale she uncovered, she felt herself being pulled deeper into its mystery.

Chapter 11

The next morning, Claire sat at the table in the cafe, her laptop open and a fresh cup of coffee in hand. She was deep into her research, scrolling through old articles and archival footage about the Ogopogo's evolution from a local legend to a regional symbol. Emily and Ellie arrived together, their voices carrying a mix of curiosity and excitement as they joined her.

"You've been busy," Emily said, glancing at Claire's screen.

"You could say that," Claire replied with a grin. "I've been digging into how Ogopogo became such a massive part of the Okanagan's identity. It's fascinating—did you know the tourism association once offered a million-dollar reward for proof of its existence?"

Emily raised her eyebrows. "A million dollars? That's some serious incentive. When was this?"

"The 1980s," Claire explained. "It was part of a campaign to boost tourism. They figured the legend of the Ogopogo was unique enough to draw people in. And they weren't wrong. The reward got international attention—scientists, cryptozoologists, and even amateur enthusiasts came to try their luck."

Ellie leaned forward, intrigued. "Did anyone actually find anything?"

Claire shook her head. "Nothing conclusive, of course. However the stories and media coverage cemented Ogopogo as a symbol of the Okanagan. It wasn't just a lake creature anymore—it became a cultural icon."

Emily sipped her tea thoughtfully. "That's clever marketing but also a little risky. What if someone had actually found proof?"

"That's where it gets interesting," Claire said. "Around the same time, Greenpeace got involved. They declared Ogopogo an endangered species, emphasizing that any search should be non-invasive. They wanted to make sure no one would harm the lake or its ecosystem in the name of finding the creature."

Ellie smiled. "So, the environmentalists turned the legend into a conservation effort. I like that angle—it adds a whole new layer of meaning to the story."

Claire nodded, scrolling through her notes. "Exactly. And it wasn't just about the Ogopogo itself. Greenpeace used it to highlight the importance of protecting the lake and its biodiversity. The million-dollar reward became less about proving Ogopogo's existence and more about preserving the mystery—and the environment."

Emily leaned back, her camera resting on the table. "It's amazing how a legend can evolve like that. From an Indigenous guardian spirit to a tourist attraction to a symbol of environmental awareness."

"Exactly," Claire said. "It shows how adaptable stories are. They change to fit the times, but they always have a core that connects people to something bigger— whether it's nature, culture, or just the thrill of the unknown."

Ellie glanced out at the shimmering lake, her expression thoughtful. "It's like the Ogopogo has become more than a creature. It's an idea—a way for people to connect to the land and its history."

The three women sat in silence for a moment, their gazes drawn to the lake's endless expanse. Somewhere out there, a mystery waited—one that had captured imaginations for centuries.

Emily broke the silence, her voice filled with determination. "I think it's time we added our own chapter to this story. Let's find out what the Ogopogo really means for everyone."

Chapter 12

The afternoon sun filtered through the trees as Claire, Emily, and Ellie pulled up to Ryan's studio in Westbank. Ryan greeted them at the door, a smudge of blue paint streaked across his forearm and a wide grin on his face.

"Back so soon?" he teased, stepping aside to let them in.

"We couldn't stay away," Claire replied with a laugh. "We've been piecing together everything we've learned about the Ogopogo, and we thought you might be able to add a bit more perspective."

Ryan wiped his hands on a cloth and gestured for them to sit near the mural he had been working on—a vibrant depiction of the lake at sunset, with faint, serpentine shadows hidden beneath the water's surface.

"You've got questions, I've got stories," Ryan said, settling into a chair across from them.

Ellie leaned forward. "We've been trying to figure out how to describe the Ogopogo—what it's like, how it moves. Can you help us paint a picture?"

Ryan nodded, his expression growing serious. "The Ogopogo isn't something you just see—it's something you feel. Let me try to describe it for you."

He paused as if pulling the memory from the depths of his mind. "Imagine standing by the lake on a quiet day. The water is still, almost glass-like when suddenly there's a shift—a ripple that shouldn't be there. You don't hear it right away, but you sense it like the lake is breathing."

Emily adjusted her camera, captivated by his words.

"Picture something massive and smooth, gliding beneath the surface," Ryan continued. "Its movement is rhythmic, like waves rolling in slow motion, but the waves aren't coming from the wind—they're alive. You'd think it was a giant snake, except its back is ridged, with humps rising and falling in perfect sequence, like the crest of a wave."

Claire shivered. "What does the skin feel like? If you could touch it, I mean."

Ryan tilted his head, considering. "Smooth, but not soft. It would have the texture of a dolphin—firm and slick but with a strength beneath the surface, like a coiled spring. And then there are the ridges—hard, almost like bone, tracing down its spine. It's not like anything else you'd find in the lake."

Ellie furrowed her brow. "And the size? How big do you think it really is?"

"Big," Ryan said simply, spreading his hands. "At least as long as a boat, maybe more. But it's not the size that gets you—it's the presence. When you see it—or feel it—you know you're not looking at an ordinary animal. It's like the lake itself has come alive like it's watching you as much as you're watching it."

The room fell silent for a moment as his words hung in the air.

"And then it's gone," Ryan added softly. "The water settles, and you're left wondering if it was even real. But deep down, you know it was. You felt it."

Claire exhaled, her voice almost a whisper. "That's incredible. It's no wonder the legend has lasted for centuries."

Emily raised her camera, snapping a shot of Ryan's mural. "I think you just gave us more than a description—you gave us a connection. It's not just a creature, it's part of the lake itself."

Ryan smiled, standing to stretch. "Exactly. That's what the Syilx people have always said. The nx̌ax̌aitkʷ isn't just a being—it's the spirit of the water. Whether you believe in the Ogopogo or not, you can't deny the power of what it represents."

As the ladies left the studio, the lake glimmering in the distance, they couldn't help but feel the weight of Ryan's words. The Ogopogo wasn't just a mystery to solve—it was a story to honor, a piece of the Okanagan's soul.

Chapter 13

The road back to Kelowna brought them over the lake's bridge, with shimmering waters stretching out in both directions. The sun hung low in the sky, casting golden streaks across the surface as if the lake itself was glowing with secrets yet to be uncovered. Claire drove, her hands steady on the wheel, while Ellie and Emily sat quietly, each lost in thought.

Finally, Claire broke the silence, her voice thoughtful. "Ryan's right, you know. You can't deny the power of what the Ogopogo represents. It's more than just a creature—it's a symbol of this place, of everything the lake and the valley stand for."

Emily glanced up from her camera. "You mean like a cultural icon? Kind of like how Bigfoot is for the Pacific Northwest?"

"Partly," Claire replied, her gaze fixed on the winding road ahead. "But it's deeper than that. Think about it. The Ogopogo isn't just about mystery or tourism. It's a thread that ties so many things together—history, nature, culture, even identity. It's this idea that the lake isn't just water. It's alive, connected to the people and the land in ways we don't fully understand."

Ellie nodded slowly. "That connection to the Syilx stories really struck me. The idea of the nx̌ax̌aitkʷ as a guardian spirit—a reminder to respect the lake and live in harmony with nature. It's not just about what's in the lake, but what it stands for."

Claire smiled faintly. "Exactly. And then you have the modern layers—how it's become a part of the valley's identity in a different way. Tourism, conservation, even science. People come here because they're drawn to the mystery, but they stay because of what this place makes them feel. It's like the Ogopogo is a mirror—it reflects back whatever you bring to it. Wonder, fear, respect, curiosity."

Emily raised her camera, snapping a photo of the lake through the car window. "It's kind of poetic when you think about it. A legend that's evolved to mean different things to different people but still holds its core—a connection to the lake, to something bigger than us."

Claire turned to glance at her. "And that's what makes it so powerful. Whether it's real or not doesn't matter as much as what it inspires in people. It's a reminder to look beyond the surface—of the lake, of life. To think about what's underneath, what connects us all."

Ellie leaned back in her seat, her expression thoughtful. "You're right. Even if it's not a real creature—it's a story. A way of understanding this place, its beauty, its mysteries. Maybe that's why it's lasted so long. Because it's not just about the lake, it's about the community, too."

The car grew quiet again, but this time, the silence felt full—of meaning, of shared understanding. The Ogopogo wasn't just a question to answer or a mystery to solve. It was a story to tell, a lesson to learn, a piece of the valley's soul that had touched them all.

Chapter 14

Ellie stood on the dock at Kelowna's City Park, her gear spread out around her—a laptop, a portable sonar scanner, and a stack of maps marked with notes and annotations. The lake stretched out before her, its surface calm and shimmering under the late afternoon sun. She adjusted the strap of her bag, her scientific mind eager to uncover the secrets hidden beneath the tranquil waters.

After loading her equipment onto a small research boat she had rented for the day, Ellie set out across the lake. Her first destination was the shelf that, according to her research, lay just off the downtown shoreline. As the boat glided away from the dock, she scanned the horizon, her trained eyes already noting subtle changes in the water's surface and current.

Once she reached her target area, Ellie lowered the sonar scanner into the lake, watching as the screen began to map the underwater terrain in real-time. The results were as striking as they were unexpected.

"It's just as I thought," she murmured to herself, jotting notes in her journal. The shelf was massive, a flat expanse of lakebed that extended out from the shoreline before plunging into the abyss. Beneath the waters of City Park, the lake dropped off dramatically, creating a sheer underwater cliff that extended hundreds of feet down.

Ellie leaned closer to the screen. "That's not natural," she muttered. "Not entirely, anyway."

She had read theories that the depth of Okanagan Lake, particularly near Kelowna, wasn't solely the result of natural glacial activity. The way the shelf abruptly ended, combined with the almost unnatural uniformity of the drop-off, suggested something more. Ancient landslides? Geological shifts? Or something else entirely?

Curious, Ellie turned the boat toward a deeper section of the lake, just beyond the shelf. Here, the sonar revealed a network of strange formations—ridges, grooves, and what looked like the remnants of an ancient underwater landscape.

"This area must have been above water at some point," she mused aloud, her fingers flying across her laptop's keyboard. "The contours, the shapes—it looks like erosion patterns you'd find on land, not underwater."

As she moved further out, the depths grew darker, the sonar revealing just how deep the lake was in its central basin—close to 800 feet. The sheer vastness of it struck her. Okanagan Lake was more than just a picturesque body of water. It was a geological wonder, holding mysteries both natural and, perhaps, unnatural.

She paused, her gaze drifting to the shoreline in the distance. Downtown Kelowna sat perched on the edge of this ancient, mysterious drop-off, a city balanced on the edge of an underwater world few had ever explored. The thought sent a chill down her spine.

After collecting her data, Ellie returned to the dock, her mind racing with possibilities. The lake wasn't just a home for myths and legends—it was a place of scientific intrigue, a place where the past and present collided beneath the surface.

As she packed up her equipment, she couldn't shake the feeling that the Ogopogo sightings were more than just stories. The unusual depths, the abrupt changes in the lakebed—it all hinted at something deeper. Perhaps the lake wasn't just hiding a creature. Perhaps it was hiding a history no one fully understood.

Chapter 15

The three women sat at a cozy corner table in the cafe, steaming drinks in hand. Claire sipped her chai latte while Emily reviewed photos on her camera. Ellie, ever the scientist, had her laptop open, ready to dive into the parallels between Okanagan Lake's Ogopogo and Scotland's famous Loch Ness Monster.

"So, tell us," Claire prompted, setting her mug down. "What's the deal with the Loch Ness Monster? Are we dealing with a cousin of Ogopogo here?"

Ellie chuckled, leaning back in her chair. "It's an interesting comparison, for sure. Both the Loch Ness Monster and the Ogopogo share a lot of similarities, but they also have key differences that make each unique."

Emily looked up, intrigued. "Alright, let's start with the similarities."

Ellie nodded. "First off, both legends are tied to large, deep lakes. Loch Ness in Scotland and Okanagan Lake here are incredibly deep—Loch Ness is over 750 feet deep, and Okanagan Lake is just shy of that in places. These depths create the perfect environment for mysteries, both real and imagined."

Claire jotted notes in her journal. "And both creatures have that serpentine, undulating description, right?"

"Exactly," Ellie confirmed. "Eyewitness accounts of both creatures describe them as long, serpent-like beings with humps or ridges that move in a wave-like motion. They're both said to travel just beneath the surface, creating ripples that people often mistake for something massive."

Emily tilted her head thoughtfully. "And the differences?"

"That's where it gets interesting," Ellie said. "Loch Ness, for example, is thought to have a colder, murkier environment than Okanagan Lake. The water visibility in Loch Ness is extremely low, making it much harder to observe or photograph anything under the surface. Okanagan Lake, by contrast, has clearer waters in some areas, which might explain why there are more claimed sightings here with slightly better visual descriptions."

Claire chimed in. "What about the cultural significance? Do the two legends hold the same kind of meaning?"

"Not quite," Ellie replied. "The Loch Ness Monster, or Nessie as it's affectionately called, became a global phenomenon in the 20th century, particularly after that infamous photo from the 1930s—the one that turned out to be a hoax. It's now one of Scotland's biggest tourist attractions. The Ogopogo, on the other hand, has a much deeper Indigenous cultural significance. The Syilx people have been telling stories about nx̌ax̌aitkʷ, the sacred spirit of the lake, long before settlers arrived."

Emily leaned forward. "So, Ogopogo is more of a guardian figure, while Nessie is more of a global curiosity?"

"Exactly," Ellie said. "Nessie's more of a spectacle—an icon for cryptozoologists and monster hunters. The Ogopogo is rooted in the identity of the Okanagan Valley. It's not just about the creature—it's about the relationship between people and the lake."

Claire tapped her pen against her notebook. "What about scientific explanations? Do they overlap?"

Ellie nodded. "Yes and no. Both creatures are often explained as misidentifications of natural phenomena. For example, sturgeon or other large fish might explain Ogopogo sightings. For Loch Ness, some theories suggest large eels or even optical illusions caused by wind patterns on the water. The difference is that Loch Ness has been far more scrutinized with things like sonar mapping and even DNA sampling, while Okanagan Lake remains less studied."

Emily grinned. "So, you're saying there's more mystery to unravel here."

Ellie smirked. "Exactly. And unlike Loch Ness, where so many of the studies have been inconclusive, Okanagan Lake still feels… untouched in a way. There's more to explore, both scientifically and culturally."

Claire closed her journal with a satisfied smile. "I think we've got our angle, The Ogopogo as more than just Canada's answer to Nessie. It's a creature, a symbol, and a story all its own."

Ellie raised her mug. "To uncovering mysteries—one ripple at a time."

Emily and Claire clinked their cups against hers, their excitement growing with each discovery.

Chapter 16

Claire pressed deeper into the dusty archives of the Kelowna Museum, the fluorescent lights flickering overhead as she sifted through boxes of brittle newspaper clippings and uncatalogued letters. The silence in the room was thick, broken only by the rustle of aging paper and the occasional creak of the floorboards.

It had been days since the team first reviewed the old photo of the mysterious vertebra, and the image had stayed with her. There was something about its sheer size and shape that haunted her thoughts. She was determined to find anything—a clue, a record, even a rumor—that might explain what had happened to the bone or where it might have gone.

At the back of a filing drawer labeled "Misc. Lake Reports - 1890s to 1940s," she discovered a yellowed envelope addressed to the Vernon Historical Society. Inside was a typed letter dated 1931:

To Whom It May Concern,
Regarding the specimen retrieved from Okanagan Lake in the 1880s (believed to be a cetacean vertebra): the object was last recorded in 1927 in a temporary exhibit at the Thompson Museum. It was removed for transport to Victoria for further study. No follow-up documentation has been found regarding its arrival. A museum staff member at the time noted the specimen bore unusual wear patterns inconsistent with marine origin.

Claire read the lines three times.

Unusual wear patterns?

She grabbed her phone and snapped a photo of the letter, then quickly jotted down the name of the museum and the date.

As she searched further, she uncovered a small leather-bound field notebook belonging to a naturalist named Edward Langford. Between sketches of birds and lake plants was an entry from July 1926:

I saw "Whalebone" again in Vernon's exhibit today. Fascinating. I'm not convinced it's from any known marine species. Possibly a large aquatic reptile? Locals dismiss it as a hoax, but something feels authentic. Will speak to curator about preservation.

Claire's pulse quickened. She knew the name Langford. He'd published a short book on Canadian inland species in the 1930s. If even a seasoned naturalist questioned the bone's origin, there was more to this story.

That evening, she met Emily, Ellie, Liam, and Ethan at their usual café spot by the waterfront. The others were already seated on the patio, watching the lake as its surface turned molten gold in the evening light.

Claire dropped the letter and the notebook on the table. "I think I found something."

Emily leaned forward, her eyes lighting up. "What is it?"

"Confirmation the bone made it to a museum in Thompson. And this notebook—a naturalist thought it might not be a whalebone at all. Possibly reptilian."

Ellie raised an eyebrow, intrigued despite herself. "That could suggest something prehistoric. Something freshwater-adapted."

Liam rubbed his jaw. "What if the bone wasn't lost? What if someone made sure it was buried—intentionally?"

"Or stolen," Ethan added. "To keep people from asking more questions."

Claire looked out at the lake, its stillness now layered with tension. "If it was part of a larger skeleton... or just one of many relics in this lake, what else is out there? And who else knows about it?"

They sat in thoughtful silence, the lake's surface rippling slightly as a breeze swept through. Below them, the water kept its secrets for now.

Chapter 17

The ladies had decided to spend the morning at Rotary Beach, a quiet spot where the breeze carried the scent of fresh water and pine. Claire stood near the shore, her toes sinking into the warm sand as she gazed out over the lake. A nostalgic smile played on her lips as she turned to Ellie and Emily, who were lounging on a nearby picnic blanket.

"You know," Claire began, her voice soft, "Coming back here reminds me of when I was a kid. My family used to vacation in Kelowna every summer, and Rotary Beach was always our first stop. I remember wading into the water here—it felt like you could walk forever, and it would only come up to your waist."

Emily perked up, setting her camera down. "Seriously? I've never been in a lake like that."

Claire laughed, nodding. "It's true. The sand beneath your feet felt so soft, and the water was always calm like it was welcoming you in. As a kid, it was the perfect place to play. No matter how many stories I heard about the Ogopogo, I never felt scared swimming here."

Ellie tilted her head, curious. "Even with the stories in the back of your mind?"

"Not at all," Claire said, shaking her head. "The stories were more like a fun mystery to me back then—something to talk about around the campfire. But the lake itself? It felt safe, almost comforting. I think the water has that effect. It's more than just a place to swim—it feels like it's alive in the best possible way."

Emily smiled. "That's beautiful, Claire. Did you ever swim anywhere else around here?"

"Oh, definitely," Claire said, her smile widening. "Gyro Beach was where all the cute guys hung out. My cousins and I would head there, pretending we weren't watching them toss frisbees or show off their muscles. It was so full of life—families, teenagers, everyone just enjoying the lake."

Ellie chuckled. "Sounds like you made the most of your time here."

"I did," Claire admitted, her voice tinged with warmth. "And then there was downtown Kelowna. I still have a picture of myself sitting on the old Ogopogo statue they had near City Park. My parents thought it was hilarious—me grinning from ear to ear on top of a creature I was supposedly afraid of."

Emily grabbed her camera, aiming it at Claire. "We need to recreate that photo. You, back on an Ogopogo statue. It's only fair."

Claire laughed, brushing her hair out of her face. "I don't think I have the balance for that anymore, but it's tempting."

Ellie glanced out at the lake, her gaze thoughtful. "It's funny, isn't it? How a place can hold so many layers of meaning? For you, the lake was a place of joy and fun. For others, it's mystery and legend. And for the Syilx people, it's sacred. Yet somehow, it's all connected."

Claire nodded, her expression softening. "That's the magic of this place. No matter who you are or what you believe, the lake has a way of pulling you in, making you feel like you're a part of its story."

The three women fell silent, each lost in their own thoughts as the water lapped gently at the shore. The lake stretched out before them, its surface shimmering under the morning sun, holding the echoes of countless memories and untold mysteries.

Chapter 18

The sun dipped low over Okanagan Lake, casting a warm glow through the windows of Ryan's studio. Claire, Emily, and Ellie sat in a semicircle around Ryan, who was preparing to share more about the Syilx people's connection to the lake and its sacred spirit, nx̌ax̌aitkʷ.

"Our stories, or captikʷɬ, have been passed down through generations," Ryan began, his voice resonant with reverence. "They teach us about our natural laws and how to live in harmony with the land and water."

He paused, allowing the weight of his words to settle. "One such story speaks of nx̌ax̌aitkʷ, the spirit of the lake. It's said that this being travels throughout the waters, caring for them and reminding us of their sacredness."

Emily leaned forward, her curiosity piqued. "Is there a specific story about nx̌ax̌aitkʷ that stands out to you?"

Ryan nodded. "Yes, there's a tale of a visiting chief who came to the lake and did not provide an offering for safe passage across the waters. In response, the spirit caused a great commotion, leading to the chief's canoe capsizing. This story serves as a reminder of the importance of respecting the natural world and the protocols that need to be followed to live in harmony with it."

Ellie listened intently, her scientific mind appreciating the depth of cultural significance. "So, nx̌ax̌aitkʷ isn't just a creature. It's a symbol of sustainability and the interconnectedness between the people, the land, and the water."

"Exactly," Ryan affirmed. "It's not something to be feared but rather respected. Our stories serve as reminders of the natural laws and protocols that need to be followed for future generations to survive in harmony with the environment."

Claire glanced at the mural Ryan had been working on—a vibrant depiction of the lake with subtle, flowing shapes beneath the surface. "Your art captures that essence beautifully," she remarked.

Ryan smiled appreciatively. "Thank you. Through my art, I aim to convey the deep respect and connection we have with nx̌ax̌aitkʷ and the waters it inhabits. It's a way to keep our stories alive and share them with others."

Emily tilted her head, her brow furrowed. "What exactly is an offering? What should someone give to the lake to show respect?"

Ryan smiled, his gaze thoughtful. "An offering is something meaningful, something given with intention. For the Syilx people, it might be tobacco, food, or even a prayer. It's not about the value of the item—it's about the act of giving, acknowledging the lake's power and our reliance on it. When you make an offering, you're not just giving to the water; you're entering into a relationship with it, one based on respect and gratitude."

Claire leaned forward, intrigued. "So, if someone were to go out on the lake today, would an offering still be expected?"

Ryan nodded. "Absolutely. The spirit of the lake hasn't changed, even if the world around it has. Giving an offering is a way to remind ourselves of that connection—to remember that the lake is more than a resource. It's a living, breathing part of our world."

Chapter 19

The morning sun spilled into the café as Claire, Emily, and Ellie gathered again. Their usual table by the window had become their unofficial headquarters, a space where theories swirled as freely as the steam from their mugs.

"I've been thinking about what Ryan said last night," Claire began, stirring her chai latte absentmindedly. "How nx̌ax̌aitkʷ is more than just a creature. It got me wondering—how many other places have similar stories?"

Ellie smirked, leaning back in her chair. "Funny you should mention that. I did some digging last night, and let me tell you, Ogopogo has a lot of company."

Emily raised an eyebrow. "Oh? Do share."

Ellie opened her laptop, pulling up a map with pins scattered across it. "Let's start close to home. There's Champ, the supposed lake monster of Lake Champlain on the border of New York, Vermont, and Quebec. Very similar descriptions to Ogopogo—long, serpentine, and always spotted just below the surface."

Claire leaned forward, intrigued. "Makes you wonder if there's some link between these stories."

"Exactly," Ellie said. "And then there's Tahoe Tessie in Lake Tahoe. Again, big, deep lake, cold water, and reports of a giant creature swimming just beneath the waves."

Emily laughed. "So, another version of the lake monster? What's its story?"

"Well," Ellie said, scrolling down, "Some legends say Tessie's sightings date back to Indigenous stories of the Washoe people. But like most of these creatures, it really gained attention in the 20th century, with boaters and swimmers claiming to see something huge in the water."

Claire tapped her pen against her notebook. "And what about other places in North America?"

Ellie grinned, clearly in her element. "Glad you asked. Flathead Lake in Montana has its own monster. People describe it as a large eel- or snake-like creature. The legend there is a little different, though—less tied to

Indigenous lore and more about modern sightings."

Emily leaned forward. "What's it called?"

"Just the Flathead Lake Monster," Ellie said with a shrug. "Not the most creative name, but the sightings are similar to Ogopogo—people seeing humps breaking the surface of the water or something moving just below."

"What about Canada?" Claire asked.

Ellie pointed to another pin on her map. "Lake Manitoba, right here in our backyard. The creature's called Manipogo, and it's described almost exactly like Ogopogo—a long, serpentine figure that swims near the surface. Some of the stories there go back over a century, with First Nations people sharing accounts of the creature."

Claire jotted down notes. "So, Manipogo could be a relative of Ogopogo. That's interesting."

Emily tilted her head. "And the Great Lakes? They're huge—there's got to be something there."

Ellie nodded. "Absolutely. Lake Erie has its own creature called Bessie. Same deal—serpent-like, often spotted by boaters. The earliest reports date back to the 18th century, so it's another long-standing legend."

Emily leaned back, her expression thoughtful. "It's fascinating how many of these creatures exist in stories around North America. And they're all so similar."

Claire smiled. "It makes you wonder if these lakes really do have something hiding in their depths or if it's just our collective imagination."

"Or maybe it's both," Ellie said, closing her laptop. "Stories like these connect us to the places we live, to the land and water."

Chapter 20

Claire arrived at the café early, already seated at their usual table with three steaming mugs in front of her when Emily and Ellie walked in. She raised one of the cups in greeting.

"Fuel for the monster hunters," she said with a grin.

Ellie slid into her seat and opened her laptop without a word, her eyes gleaming with excitement. The screen glowed with a sprawling digital map covered in multicolored pins. "I couldn't stop after North America," she said, barely able to contain herself. "Turns out, we're not the only ones with lake monster legends. There's a whole world of them."

Emily sat down slowly, intrigued. "Show us."

Claire leaned forward, "Alright, let's hear it. Where are we headed first?"

"Scotland," Ellie began, pulling up a picture of a misty lake. "But not Loch Ness. There's another lake monster—Morag, from Loch Morar. It's one of Scotland's deepest lakes, even deeper than Loch Ness. Morag is described as similar to Nessie—large, humpbacked, and serpent-like—but less famous. Sightings go back centuries, with local lore tying it to the spirit of the lake."

Emily raised an eyebrow. "So, Scotland has two monsters? I didn't know that."

"Yep," Ellie said. "And the vibe is different. Morag feels more like an echo of ancient times, while Nessie has become more of a tourist icon."

"Interesting," Claire mused. "Where to next?"

"Russia," Ellie said, pulling up a photo of Lake Brosno. "This one's called the Brosno Dragon. It's said to inhabit Lake Brosno, and the stories date back to the Middle Ages. Some describe it as a dragon, others as a prehistoric reptile. Legends even claim it capsized boats and swallowed horses."

Emily laughed. "So, it's got a bit more bite than Morag or Nessie."

"Definitely," Ellie agreed. "But again, no solid evidence. The lake is remote and hard to study, which adds to the mystery."

"And the next one?" Claire asked.

"Lake Garda in Italy," Ellie said, scrolling to another pin. "They call the creature Bennie. It's described as a huge, snake-like creature spotted by fishermen and boaters. It's not as famous as Nessie or Ogopogo, but the sightings are just as compelling. And Lake Garda is the largest lake in Italy, so there's plenty of space for a mystery to hide."

Claire leaned back, taking it all in. "Europe seems to love its lake monsters. What about the rest of the world?"

Ellie nodded, flipping to another part of the map. "Asia has some fascinating ones. Lake Tianchi, or Heaven Lake, is on the border between China and North Korea, and it has the Tianchi Monster. It's said to look like a dinosaur, with sightings going back hundreds of years. The lake itself is a volcanic crater, which adds another layer of mystery."

"That's wild," Emily said. "And Japan?"

"Lake Ikeda," Ellie replied. "Their monster is called Issie, a giant black creature with a serpentine body. It's not as widely reported as some of the others, but local legends tie it to the lake's spirit, much like nx̌ax̌aitkʷ."

Claire tapped her pen against her notebook. "And Africa? Any legends there?"

Ellie smiled. "Absolutely. Lake Victoria, Africa's largest lake, has a creature called Lukwata. It's described as a serpent, with stories deeply rooted in local myths. Then there's Lake Tele in the Republic of Congo, home to stories of Mokele-Mbembe. This one's more famous as a dinosaur-like creature often said to inhabit both rivers and lakes. It's considered more of a land-and-water hybrid than a pure lake monster."

Emily raised her camera, capturing a picture of the map on Ellie's screen. "It's incredible how similar all these creatures are. Huge, serpent-like, tied to deep lakes or ancient stories."

Claire nodded. "And yet, they're all unique, reflecting the culture and landscape of where they come from. It makes you wonder if they're all connected somehow—or if they're just part of something universal in human imagination."

Ellie closed her laptop, a thoughtful expression on her face. "Whether they're real or not, these creatures tell us something about ourselves. They're about mystery, respect for nature, and the stories we create to explain the unknown."

Claire smiled. "And it seems like every lake monster, from Ogopogo to Mokele-Mbembe, carries a bit of that magic."

The women sipped their drinks in silence, their thoughts drifting to the countless lakes and stories waiting to be explored.

Chapter 21

The familiar clink of mugs and chatter of patrons filled the cafe as Claire, Emily, and Ellie settled into their now-regular routine of delving into the world's lake legends. Ellie had brought another map. This one dotted with pins marking South America and Australia.

"Okay," Ellie began, opening her laptop and pulling up her notes. "We've covered North America, Europe, Asia, and Africa. But South America and Australia have their share of mysterious creatures, too."

Emily leaned forward, her camera in hand. "Alright, hit us with it. What's lurking in the lakes down there?"

"Let's start with Peru," Ellie said, pointing to a pin on the Amazon Basin. "There's a creature called Yacumama, which means 'Mother of the Water.' It's said to be a giant serpent-like creature that lives in the lakes and waterways of the Amazon. Local legends describe it as so massive that it can create whirlpools and suck in anything that gets too close."

Claire raised an eyebrow. "A mother figure? That's different from the usual terrifying monster angle."

"Exactly," Ellie agreed. "The Yacumama is seen as a powerful and protective force, but also dangerous if disrespected. It's a reminder of how interconnected the Amazon's ecosystem is—and how humans are just a small part of it."

Emily jotted notes. "And Argentina?"

Ellie smiled, scrolling to another pin. "Lake Nahuel Huapi, in Patagonia. The creature there is called Nahuelito, and it's described as a giant serpent or dinosaur-like being. Like Nessie and Ogopogo, the sightings are sporadic but consistent enough to keep the legend alive. Some even think Nahuelito could be a plesiosaur."

"Another prehistoric tie," Claire said, nodding. "Interesting. What's the vibe around Nahuelito? Is it more of a tourist attraction or cultural symbol?"

"Both," Ellie replied. "It's part of the local identity, but it's also a curiosity that draws in visitors. Much like Ogopogo, it bridges the line between mystery and marketing."

Emily laughed. "Alright, now let's head to Australia. What's swimming down under?"

Ellie pointed to the Hawkesbury River, just north of Sydney. "This one's called the Hawkesbury River Monster. It's often described as a prehistoric, plesiosaur-like creature, and the sightings date back to Aboriginal stories. Modern reports usually come from fishermen who claim to see something massive moving through the water."

Claire tapped her pen against her mug. "Another plesiosaur? That's becoming a theme."

"It really is," Ellie said. "But the Hawkesbury River Monster has a twist. The area is known for deep, interconnected waterways, which adds to the mystery of where such a creature could hide."

"And the last one?" Claire asked.

Ellie moved her cursor to a pin near Lake Alexandrina in South Australia. "The Muldjewangk. This one is deeply rooted in Aboriginal folklore. It's said to be a dangerous water creature that inhabits the lake and surrounding waterways. The stories warn against going into certain areas of the water, where the Muldjewangk is believed to drag people under."

Emily's eyes widened. "That's intense. So, it's more of a warning legend?"

"Exactly," Ellie said. "It's less about curiosity and more about teaching respect for the water. Aboriginal stories often emphasize the spiritual connection to the land, and the Muldjewangk reflects that. It's a reminder that not everything is ours to explore or control."

Claire leaned back in her chair, her expression thoughtful. "It's amazing how these creatures are tied so closely to the cultures and landscapes they come from."

Ellie nodded. "And that's the thread connecting all these stories. Whether it's Yacumama in the Amazon, Nahuelito in Argentina, or the Muldjewangk in Australia, they're not just legends—they're reflections of how we see and respect the world around us."

Emily raised her camera, snapping a photo of Ellie and Claire deep in discussion. "This might be my favorite discovery yet. These creatures aren't just fascinating—they're meaningful."

Claire smiled. "And now we've got a global map of mysteries to explore. Maybe the Ogopogo isn't alone after all."

Chapter 22

"Why are lake monster legends everywhere?" Claire asked, breaking the silence as she flipped through a notepad filled with scribbled lines and underlined names. "Scotland, Japan, the U.S., here in the Okanagan... different cultures, different timelines, but the same types of sightings. There has to be something connecting them."

The clatter of a coffee cup being set on the table punctuated her question. The three women sat at their now-familiar corner table at the café, tucked beneath a faded black-and-white photograph of Kelowna's shoreline from the 1920s. The café had become their headquarters, a low-key war room for piecing together centuries of folklore and science.

Ellie looked up from her laptop, where she had been cross-referencing topographical maps and geological charts. "I think part of it is psychological. Humans have always been fascinated—and terrified—by what lies beneath. Lakes are deep, dark, and often uncharted. That makes them the perfect stage for monsters."

Emily sipped her tea, her camera resting on the seat beside her. "But it's not just imagination. These legends persist across continents. There are sightings, drawings, carvings—some dating back thousands of years. It's not just fear of the unknown. It's recognition of something they all experienced."

Claire nodded slowly. "Maybe it's not just cultural myth. Maybe it's a shared human memory—or even a shared creature."

Ellie raised an eyebrow. "You mean like a global species, scattered and surviving in deep lakes around the world?"

Claire leaned forward. "Exactly. What if Ogopogo, Nessie, and the others are all part of the same story? Same origin. Different lakes."

Emily looked between them. "That would explain a lot. But it would also mean they've either adapted to separate ecosystems... or there's a connection between the lakes themselves. Underground channels, maybe?"

"Or even something more ancient," Ellie said thoughtfully. "A time when freshwater bodies were connected in ways we no longer understand. The fossil record is incomplete. We know that."

Claire tapped her pen against her notebook.

Ellie finally said, "I think we're not chasing a creature. We're chasing a truth that's been half-forgotten. Something hidden in stories, science, and symbols. We just have to read between the ripples."

Emily raised her camera, aiming it at Claire and Ellie as they pored over the maps. "Say cheese, conspiracy theorists."

Claire laughed. "We're not conspiracy theorists. We're researchers."

"Same difference," Emily teased, snapping the photo.

Ellie tapped her laptop screen, which displayed a map marked with all the lakes they'd discussed. "Let's start with the basics. Lake depth. Almost every one of these lakes is incredibly deep. Loch Ness, for example, is over 750 feet deep. Okanagan Lake is nearly 800 feet in its central basin. These depths make it easy to imagine something large hiding down there, out of sight."

Emily nodded, scribbling in her own journal. "And it's not just the depth. Many of these lakes are old—like prehistoric old.

They've existed for tens of thousands, if not millions, of years. Plenty of time for creatures to evolve or for myths to take root."

Claire leaned forward. "What about the geology? Any patterns there?"

Ellie nodded. "Definitely. A lot of these lakes are glacial or volcanic in origin. Take Lake Tianchi, for example—it's a volcanic crater lake. Okanagan Lake and Loch Ness were both carved out by glaciers. These geological processes create unique underwater environments—hidden caves, shelves, and deep basins—that could easily hide something unusual."

"And the sightings?" Claire asked. "Do people describe the creatures the same way?"

"Pretty much," Ellie said. "Long, serpent-like bodies, often with humps or ridges. Movement is usually undulating, like a snake or eel. Some, like Nessie and Nahuelito, are described as having a dinosaur-like appearance—maybe a plesiosaur. Others, like Yacumama and the Brosno Dragon, lean more toward the mythical, described as enormous snakes or dragons."

Emily chuckled. "So, basically, people see what fits their imagination or their culture's stories."

"Exactly," Ellie agreed. "And that brings us to another connection, cultural significance. Every lake monster has a story tied to the people and history of its region. For example, nx̌ax̌aitkʷ is more than just a creature—it's a guardian spirit for the Syilx people, representing respect for the lake. The Yacumama in Peru is seen as a protector of the Amazon's waterways. These aren't just monsters—they're symbols."

Claire nodded thoughtfully. "And then there's the practical side—tourism. Once the stories gain traction, they start drawing people in. Look at Loch Ness or even Ogopogo. The legends become part of the local identity, something to celebrate and market."

Emily leaned back, her eyes narrowing as she pieced it together. "So, we're looking at deep, ancient lakes, often with unusual underwater features. Creatures that are universally described in similar ways. And legends that tie into both culture and tourism. It's like all these places share the same blueprint for a mystery."

Ellie smiled. "Exactly. But here's the twist. Even with all these connections, each legend feels unique. Ogopogo isn't Nessie, and Nessie isn't the Yacumama. They're shaped by their environments, their histories, and the people who tell their stories."

Claire tapped her pen against her notebook, her mind racing. "So, what does that mean for Ogopogo? Is it just another entry on the map, or is there something here that sets it apart?"

Ellie's gaze drifted to the window, where the shimmering expanse of Okanagan Lake stretched out in the distance. "Maybe it's both. Ogopogo is part of a larger pattern, sure. But it's also part of this place—this lake, this culture. That's what makes it special."

Chapter 23

The clink of cutlery and hum of conversation filled the café as Claire, Emily, and Ellie huddled once again around their usual table. Laptops were open, notebooks scattered, and half-finished pastries sat forgotten as they leaned into their work. The trio was deep in discussion about their global lake monster map when a voice broke through the warm chatter.

"Still chasing shadows, ladies?"

The words came from a man seated alone at a nearby table, a steaming espresso in hand and an amused smirk on his face. He looked to be in his early fifties, with salt-and-pepper hair, square glasses, and a tweed blazer that screamed "historian." He closed the thick book in front of him and stood, walking slowly over to them.

"You've been making quite the spectacle here lately. Maps, photos, old news clippings... You've practically taken over the corner."

Claire's brow furrowed. "Do we know you?"

"Name's Malcolm Rowe," he replied, offering a hand that no one reached for. "Historian. And a contributor to the Kelowna Historical Quarterly. More importantly, someone who appreciates facts over folklore."

Emily crossed her arms. "And?"

Malcolm chuckled. "And I've been listening to your little project for days now. Ogopogo, ancient bones, global monster theories. It's cute. Makes for a good ghost story. But it's not journalism."

Claire bristled. "We're investigating local legends tied to scientific phenomena, history, and cultural heritage. It's not fiction."

"Isn't it?" Malcolm asked, raising an eyebrow. "Every few years, someone trots out this story with a new theory—underwater tunnels. Prehistoric survivors. Giant bones. And then? Nothing. Because there's nothing there. It's a myth, spun for tourism."

Ellie leaned forward, her voice calm but firm. "With respect, myths are often rooted in real events. Just because something hasn't been explained doesn't mean it never existed."

Malcolm smirked. "You sound like you're prepping a TED Talk, not a research paper. What's next? Atlantis in Okanagan Lake?"

Claire's cheeks flushed, but her voice stayed steady. "We're not claiming answers. We're asking questions. Something journalism used to be about."

Malcolm tapped the edge of her notebook. "Then ask better ones. Because right now, you're doing a disservice to the real history of this valley."

With that, he turned and returned to his table, flipping open his book again with theatrical flair. The girls sat in stunned silence for a moment.

Emily let out a breath. "Wow. That guy needs decaf."

Claire, however, wasn't laughing. "He's going to try to discredit us publicly. He's well-connected. And the Quarterly has a loyal readership."

Ellie shrugged. "Then we prove him wrong. Let's double-check every source. Track the bone's trail even further. Get sonar scans. Interviews. Make it undeniable."

Emily lifted her camera. "And maybe next time, we publish before he does. Let him try to dismiss us when the facts are staring him in the face."

Claire met her friends' eyes, the flame of determination igniting. "We're not backing down. Let's give them something they can't ignore."

Outside the café, a breeze swept across the lake, sending small ripples across its surface.

And somewhere beneath, the mystery waited.

Chapter 24

The afternoon sun shimmered off the lake's surface as Liam guided his sleek, restored wooden boat away from the dock. Emily sat up front, camera ready, while Claire and Ellie took their spots near the center, shaded beneath the small awning. Ethan sat beside Liam, eyes on the horizon, the mood light as the boat sliced through the calm blue expanse.

"I never get tired of this view," Claire said, stretching her legs out and lifting her face to the breeze.

"It's a postcard every day," Emily agreed, already snapping photos of the shoreline and the shifting light.

They were a good few kilometers from shore when the calm was broken. Without warning, the water under the boat lurched.

The bow pitched upward, then dropped suddenly, causing Ellie to grip the side rail. Emily's camera jolted from her hands, and Claire stumbled backward, catching herself on the seat.

"What the hell was that?" Claire shouted, her heart racing.

Emily's face paled. "Did we hit something? Did something hit us?"

The boat rocked again—not violently, but in a slow, deliberate rhythm as if the lake itself had begun to breathe.

Liam steadied the wheel. "Everyone sit tight. We're not sinking. We're just experiencing something I was hoping we wouldn't today."

"Which is?" Ellie asked, gripping the side as another ripple rolled beneath them.

Liam exhaled, slowing the motor. "A seiche."

Claire blinked. "A what now?"

Liam turned, his face more serious than they'd seen it all day. "A seiche. It's a standing wave. Happens when the water in a lake starts to rock back and forth. Think of it like what happens when you slosh water in a bathtub. It's caused by things like wind, pressure shifts, even small tremors underground. Okanagan Lake is long and narrow—perfect for it."

"But there's no wind," Emily said, her voice still tense. "And that movement felt wrong."

"That's the eerie part," Liam said. "Sometimes they hit with no warning. You don't need a storm. The energy just… builds. Then boom, the lake moves. And it doesn't stop right away. It can go for hours."

Ethan stood now, peering over the edge. The water rippled again, long, low swells that rolled unnaturally toward the shore. "It felt like something was pushing us from beneath."

Ellie narrowed her eyes. "That's what makes them so unsettling. To people who don't know what they are, seiches can look—and feel—like something supernatural. Or… something alive."

Claire shivered. "No wonder people report sightings. You feel this, and your mind goes right to Ogopogo."

Emily retrieved her camera from the floor, still shaken. "I thought something hit us."

Liam nodded. "You're not the first. Or the last. I've talked to old-timers who swear they saw the lake move like it was breathing. Some say it's Ogopogo. Others think it's the lake remembering something ancient."

They all grew quiet, watching the gentle but persistent motion beneath them.

Ellie finally broke the silence. "Seiches explain a lot of the water's strange behavior.

Not everything, but it's one piece of the puzzle."

Claire pulled out her notebook, though her hands were still shaking. "Let's say someone is on the lake alone, like that tourist. It's quiet, and then this happens. I'd freak out, too. Especially if it's at night."

"And if something was in the water..." Emily trailed off.

Liam started the motor again, slowly guiding the boat back toward shore. "Seiches are natural, sure. But when you're in the middle of one, it doesn't feel natural. It feels like the lake is warning you."

Back at the dock, the sun had dipped lower, casting long shadows across the rippling surface. The group disembarked in silence, glancing back at the deceptively calm lake.

Whatever had just happened, it had reminded them all, this lake had moods. And secrets. And sometimes, it whispered warnings in waves.

Chapter 25

Claire sat at Ethan's kitchen table, the soft glow of her laptop casting shadows across the room. The air was quiet, broken only by the occasional sound of the vineyard workers outside her window. She had been buried in research for hours, sifting through articles, images, and scientific studies. Something she remembered Ellie mentioning.

"Plesiosaur," she murmured, scrolling through a detailed illustration of the ancient marine reptile. The creature's long neck, streamlined body, and flipper-like appendages were uncannily similar to the descriptions of Ogopogo and other lake monsters around the world.

Her notes sprawled across the table, each one connecting the dots between the legend of Ogopogo and the prehistoric creature. "It's almost too perfect," she muttered, jotting down a thought. "If something like this ever lived in Okanagan Lake—or anywhere, really—it would explain so much."

Emily and Liam walked in, both with a steaming travel mug of coffee in their hands.

Emily glanced at Claire's screen, raising an eyebrow. "Deep dive into prehistoric reptiles?"

Claire smirked, pushing her reading glasses up the bridge of her nose. "You could say that. The plesiosaur is fascinating. It's the closest thing to Ogopogo in terms of physical description. Long neck, humps breaking the water's surface, undulating movement. It's almost like the sightings are echoes of something ancient."

Emily leaned over, studying the screen. "But weren't these things marine animals? How would one end up in a freshwater lake?"

"That's the tricky part," Claire admitted. "Most paleontologists agree that plesiosaurs couldn't survive in freshwater for long. Their ecosystems were completely different. But the lake's age, depth, and glacial history make it an intriguing habitat for anything that could adapt."

Emily's brow furrowed as she took a sip of her coffee. "So, you're saying Ogopogo could be a living plesiosaur?"

"Not necessarily," Claire replied, her tone measured. "But the similarities are hard to ignore. The way people describe it—the humps, the neck, the movement—it lines up perfectly. It might not be a plesiosaur, but something with similar traits could have evolved here."

Emily straightened, crossing her arms. "And what about food? What would a creature that big eat?"

Claire paused, tapping her pen against her notebook. "Good question. There are plenty of fish species in the lake—kokanee salmon, rainbow trout."

Emily's expression darkened as her mind wandered. "What if… what if they don't just eat fish? What if there's more to the disappearances on the lake than we thought?"

Claire looked up, startled. "What do you mean?"

Emily hesitated, her voice dropping to a near whisper. "I'm just saying—if something that big existed, it wouldn't be choosy about its meals. And all those stories about people disappearing on the lake… maybe they weren't accidents."

The room fell silent, the weight of her words settling between them. The soft sound of the wind blowing against the shutters suddenly seemed ominous, as if it held secrets they weren't ready to uncover.

Claire shook her head, trying to dispel the chill creeping down her spine. "Let's not jump to conclusions. We don't have any evidence of that."

Emily nodded slowly, but the unease in her eyes remained. "Still, it makes you wonder, doesn't it? What's really out there."

As the clock ticked into the late hours of the evening, Claire returned to her research, but Emily's words lingered in her mind. The legend of Ogopogo had always been about mystery and wonder. Now, it felt darker—like they were tiptoeing around something far more dangerous than they'd imagined.

Chapter 26

The morning sunlight glinted off Okanagan Lake, the water calm and clear as a light breeze rustled the leaves of the perfectly manicured trees lining the shore. Twelve-year-old Maya Lawrence leaned against the glass railing of the second-story balcony, her light golden curls catching in the wind. Below her, the sprawling backyard stretched down to the water, a private dock extending into the shimmering lake.

The house she called home was nothing short of spectacular. A modern architectural masterpiece, it featured towering glass windows, sleek lines, and a patio with a luxurious infinity pool that seemed to spill directly into the lake. The backyard was a playground for the rich, dotted with every lake toy imaginable, jet skis, paddleboards, kayaks, and even a gleaming white cabin cruiser docked at the water's edge.

Despite the glamour around her, Maya's favorite spot was the dock. The noise of parties her parents hosted, or the hum of jet skis zipping across the lake often faded into the background when she sat there, feet dangling over the edge, her thoughts focused on the water.

She padded barefoot down the stone steps that led from the house to the dock, her journal tucked under one arm. Her parents were inside, distracted as usual—her father engrossed in work calls, her mother discussing the next charity gala over coffee. They rarely noticed when Maya disappeared, and she preferred it that way. The lake was hers, a world they didn't quite understand.

Maya settled onto the dock, her toes brushing the cool surface of the water. She opened her journal, flipping to the pages filled with sketches of long, sinuous creatures gliding through the depths. Her drawings were detailed, her imagination capturing every ridge and ripple she'd seen—or thought she'd seen—beneath the surface.

"You're not a monster," she said softly as if speaking directly to the lake. "They just don't understand you."

The lake had been her constant companion since she was old enough to walk. While her parents viewed it as a status symbol, a backdrop for summer parties and Instagram-perfect photos, Maya saw it differently. To her, it was alive. She had felt its presence in the way the waves lapped against the dock, the way the light played across its surface, and in the silent moments when it seemed to watch her as much as she watched it.

When she was eight, she had her first encounter. She'd been sitting alone on the dock at sunset, her legs dangling over the edge, when the water rippled unnaturally, breaking the stillness. She had leaned forward, curious, and caught sight of it—a long, dark shadow gliding just beneath the surface. The ridges along its back had glimmered in the fading light before it disappeared. She hadn't been afraid. Instead, she felt a strange sense of calm, as if the lake was acknowledging her.

Since that day, she had been certain that Ogopogo wasn't a monster. It was misunderstood, a creature as much a part of the lake as the fish and the rocks beneath it. Her parents dismissed her stories as childish fantasies, too preoccupied with their busy lives to care. But Maya didn't mind. The lake understood her, even if they didn't.

Today, as she sketched another drawing, a ripple broke the water just a few feet away. Maya froze, her pencil hovering over the page. The ripple expanded outward, the water shimmering in the morning light. She leaned forward, her heart pounding with excitement. For a moment, she thought she saw a shadow—a long, sinuous shape moving beneath the surface.

"Maya!" her mother's voice rang out from the house, cutting through the stillness. "Breakfast is ready! Come inside before it gets cold!"

Maya sighed, closing her journal and standing. She glanced back at the water, her voice barely above a whisper. "I'll be back later. Promise."

As she made her way up the steps, the grandeur of her home in front of her a stark contrast to the quiet mystery of the lake. She paused at the top of the stairs, looking back at the dock and the rippling water beyond. To everyone else, it was just a lake. To Maya, it was something far greater—a secret worth protecting.

Chapter 27

The lake was unusually quiet that morning, a silvery mist clinging to the surface like breath on a mirror. From her small cabin porch, a local woman named Theresa Moreau sipped her coffee and stared at the shoreline with a furrowed brow. Her golden retriever, Max, had run down to the dock an hour ago and hadn't come back. He never wandered.

She called for him again. "Max! Come, boy!"

Silence. Then, a faint, echoing splash.

Theresa stood her instincts tight with unease. As she walked down the slope toward the water, she noticed the empty leash lying tangled near the boat ramp, its clasp broken.

Later that afternoon, emergency crews responded to a capsized fishing boat near Squally Point. A father and son had set out for a quiet morning on the lake. Only the son made it back, found clinging to a life jacket, teeth chattering, eyes wide with shock.

"It came out of nowhere," he kept repeating. "The boat just lifted. Like something pushed it. My dad... he fell over. I tried to grab him... then the waves... I didn't see him again."

Local divers scoured the area. No sign of the man.

Within twenty-four hours, three more incidents were reported, a pair of kayaks found adrift without their paddles, a motion-activated camera at a lakeside cabin capturing strange thrashing in the shallows just before 3 a.m., and a sonar team hired by a private researcher posting grainy images that suggested something large and moving beneath the surface—but too deep to classify.

Word spread fast.

Claire stood with Ellie, Emily, Liam, and Ethan at the edge of the marina, where local authorities had cordoned off access to one of the boat launches. News crews had arrived. The lake was no longer just a subject of quiet speculation—it was front-page, late-night, everyone-talking-about-it news.

"That's the third overturned vessel in two weeks," Ethan said, his voice low. "This isn't a coincidence."

Ellie shook her head, reviewing the sonar images on her tablet. "These disturbances are too concentrated. Too erratic. This is not normal lake behavior."

Emily turned pale. "What if it's Ogopogo? What if something scared it—or woke it?"

Claire looked out at the lake, its smooth surface now betraying nothing. "Or what if someone—or something—doesn't want us digging deeper."

A gust of wind picked up, sending a low, hollow moan through the pine trees.

Ellie slowly lowered her tablet. "We need to be careful. Whatever is happening out there... it's escalating."

The five stood in silence as the sun dipped low, the lake bathed in golden light. Beautiful. Calm.

And watching.

Chapter 28

The hum of the cafe's mid-morning crowd filled the air as Claire and Emily spread out their notes and laptops across their usual table by the window. Fresh hot drinks sat between them, untouched as they dove into their latest line of inquiry.

"I don't even know where to start," Claire admitted, scrolling through an old newspaper archive on her laptop. "Okanagan Lake has seen so many incidents over the years—drownings, boating accidents, missing people. How do we figure out which ones are just tragedies and which might be connected to… something else?"

Emily leaned back in her chair, frowning as she flipped through a printout of headlines. "It's not just about accidents. It's the strange ones—the disappearances during calm weather, the boats found adrift with no one on board. That's where the pattern might be."

Claire nodded, jotting a note in her journal. "Okay, so we focus on the unexplained. What do we know so far?"

Emily pushed her notes toward Claire. "I found a few cases that stood out like this one—1961, a man named Roger Barker. He went out fishing on a perfectly clear day near Rattlesnake Island. His boat was found the next morning, engine off, drifting near the shore. No sign of Roger. Witnesses onshore said they saw strange ripples around his boat as if something was circling it."

Claire's pen paused mid-note. "Ripples? It could be natural, but still... weird. What else?"

"Here's another," Emily said, flipping to a new page. "1987. A group of teenagers went night swimming near City Park. Two of them swam out farther than the others and disappeared. The search team found no bodies, no clues—just their towels still on the beach. The local papers ran headlines about Ogopogo for weeks."

"Classic sensationalism," Claire muttered, though her tone betrayed her unease. "Anything more recent?"

Emily nodded, her brow furrowing as she read another report. "2014. A kayaker named

Sarah Landry went missing during a solo trip near Fintry. Her kayak washed ashore two days later, completely intact. No signs of struggle. The search-and-rescue team said the water was unusually calm that day."

Claire leaned back in her chair, tapping her pen against her notebook. "It's like these stories all have one thing in common—calm conditions, no witnesses, and no solid evidence. Just empty boats and unanswered questions."

Emily glanced out the window at the lake, its surface glittering in the sunlight. "Do you think it's possible... that there's something more to these disappearances? Something not human?"

Claire hesitated, her scientific mind wrestling with the implications. "I don't know. It could just be a coincidence—an unfortunate mix of human error and natural phenomena. But some of these details don't add up."

Emily's gaze remained fixed on the water. "What if the lake isn't just dangerous? What if it's hiding something—or someone—that doesn't want to be found?"

Claire scribbled a few final notes, her pen moving quickly as her thoughts raced. "Let's focus on the locations next. If there's a pattern to where these incidents happen, it might point us toward an explanation."

As the two women settled into their research, the lake stretched out beyond the café window, its depths vast and unknowable. The surface glimmered serenely in the sunlight, but beneath it lay a history of unanswered questions and stories that refused to be forgotten.

Chapter 29

Ellie sat at the desk in her room, the soft glow of her computer screen illuminating her focused expression. She had spent the better part of the morning delving into the geological history of the Okanagan Valley, particularly the origins of Okanagan Lake and the remnants of ancient volcanic activity in the region.

Her research began with Mount Boucherie, a prominent landmark in West Kelowna. Once a towering stratovolcano active nearly 60 million years ago during the Paleocene epoch, it now stood as a weathered sentinel overlooking the lake. Erosion from multiple glacial periods had sculpted it into its current form, exposing rhyolite, andesite, and dacite formations that told a story of fiery eruptions and geological upheaval.

Transitioning to the lake's formation, Ellie discovered that Okanagan Lake is classified as a fjord lake carved by repeated glaciations. The immense weight and movement of glaciers over millennia had gouged deep valleys, which, upon the glaciers' retreat, filled with meltwater, giving birth to the lake. This glacial activity also deposited sediments, creating the rich agricultural terraces that now support the region's vineyards and orchards.

Ellie noted the intricate network of creeks and rivers that fed into Okanagan Lake. Major tributaries included Mission Creek, Vernon Creek, Trout Creek, and Penticton Creek, each contributing to the lake's volume and ecological diversity. Mission Creek, in particular, stood out as the largest tributary, producing 28% of the flow in the basin.

The lake's outflow was equally fascinating. At its southern end in Penticton, a controlled canal directed water into Skaha Lake. From there, the Okanagan River continued its journey southward, eventually crossing into Washington State and merging with the Columbia River. This transboundary water system underscored the importance of cooperative water management between Canada and the United States.

Ellie was intrigued by the human engineering that managed these natural waterways. A concrete dam at Penticton regulated the outflow from Okanagan Lake, maintaining water levels to balance flood control, water supply, and environmental concerns. This dam was part of a broader system extending from Kalamalka Lake to Osoyoos Lake, including multiple dams, vertical drop structures, and engineered channels designed to manage the region's water resources effectively.

As Ellie compiled her findings, she pondered how this geological and hydrological backdrop might intersect with their investigation into the lake's mysteries. The depths carved by ancient glaciers, the hidden underwater caves, and the complex flow of tributaries and outflows could all play roles in the enigmatic events surrounding Okanagan Lake.

She made a note to discuss these insights with Claire and Emily, considering how the lake's formation and the remnants of volcanic activity might contribute to the legends and unexplained occurrences they were exploring.

With a satisfied sigh, Ellie saved her research and prepared to share her discoveries, eager to see how this new geological perspective might shed light on the secrets lurking beneath the lake's serene surface.

Chapter 30

The projector hummed softly in one of the dimly lit meeting rooms of the University of British Columbia's Okanagan Campus (UBCO). Charts and maps glowed on the wall, bathed in a faint bluish light. Ellie stood at the front, her eyes gleaming with a mix of hesitation and fascination.

"What I'm about to propose," she began, glancing at Claire, Emily, Liam, and Ethan seated before her, "Isn't mainstream science—yet. But the data speaks for itself."

She clicked to the next slide—a topographical map of the Okanagan Valley overlayed with retreat patterns from the last glacial maximum.

"Roughly 12,000 years ago, the Cordilleran Ice Sheet covered this entire region. As it retreated, it carved out the Okanagan Valley and left behind what we now know as Okanagan Lake."

Emily leaned forward. "So, what are we looking at?"

"Glacial scars, buried subglacial tunnels, meltwater chambers." Ellie pointed to several deep blue markings on the map. "These are depressions formed as the ice retreated. In some cases, they were sealed off, buried in silt, or trapped beneath layers of glacial till. Cold, isolated, oxygen-deprived pockets."

Claire frowned. "You think something was trapped down there?"

"Not just something."

Ellie clicked again. Images filled the screen, frozen insects revived from Siberian permafrost, ancient nematodes woken after 30,000 years, and even fish embryos preserved in glacial lakes.

"Cryo-preservation is real. We've brought microscopic life back from Ice Age stasis. So, what if... and hear me out... something larger survived?"

Liam crossed his arms, his brows narrowing. "Like what? An egg?"

Ellie nodded. "A reptilian aquatic egg, possibly prehistoric. Maybe laid by something like a Plesiosaur before the Ice Age, frozen before hatching, sealed in a subglacial cave or sediment pocket. When the glacier melted, it was buried—preserved by the lake's cold depths. Until something disturbed it."

Ethan shifted uncomfortably. "You think this egg... hatched? Recently?"

Ellie pulled up a sonar scan taken six months prior. "This ridge here—Rattlesnake Ridge. A minor landslide occurred right around the same time sonar anomalies and sightings started increasing. The depth collapse might have breached a cryo-pocket."

Emily's skin prickled. "You're saying something ancient—something that's never been a part of our ecosystem—was released into the lake?"

"Not released," Ellie said. "Born. Hatched. And possibly alone, scared, disoriented. Until now."

The room fell quiet.

Claire finally spoke, her tone measured. "Ogopogo has been talked about for over a century. But what if some of those sightings weren't of the same creature—what if they were glimpses of something... and this recent wave is something new?"

Liam tapped a finger against the table. "You think it's not the legend we're chasing but a new chapter of it. A biological echo."

Ellie nodded slowly. "A ripple through time. Something that wasn't meant to survive—but did. Not supernatural. Just ancient, rare... and deeply misunderstood."

Outside, the wind stirred the trees, and the lake—not visible through the meeting room's window—glinted beneath the weight of dusk.

The ice may have melted. But perhaps, just perhaps, it had left something behind.

Chapter 31

Maya sat curled up in her bedroom window seat, her journal open on her lap. The golden light of the setting sun streamed through the floor-to-ceiling windows, casting warm shadows across her luxurious room. Her thoughts drifted to the lake as they often did, her pencil sketching the familiar serpentine shape she believed she had seen so many times.

The faint hum of voices wafted up from the open patio doors below. Curious, Maya closed her journal and crept toward the balcony. Her bare feet were silent against the polished wood as she leaned over the railing, straining to hear the conversation.

"…so they're digging into the deaths on the lake?" her father's voice said, low and steady.

"What do they think they're going to find? Ghost stories?"

Another voice replied, deeper and unfamiliar. "Not just ghost stories. Claire Bennett and Emily Fraser from the Kelowna Capital News are sniffing around, tying the Ogopogo legend to some of the disappearances. It's sensational, and they know it. If they can spin this right, it'll be a headline-grabber."

Maya's stomach twisted. She gripped the railing tighter, her golden curls blowing in the breeze.

Her father chuckled, the sound humorless. "That's all we need—more tourists trying to 'catch' the monster or, worse, people thinking it's dangerous. We've built this community on the lake's beauty, not its myths. If their story makes it to print, it could tarnish everything."

The deeper voice replied, "We can lean on the editor. There's still time to kill the article if it doesn't fit the paper's narrative."

Maya's breath caught. The Ogopogo wasn't a monster. It wasn't dangerous. It was the guardian of the lake, the silent protector that had watched over these waters for generations. How could anyone accuse it of harming people?

Anger bubbled in her chest as she listened to her father and his guest casually discuss manipulating the truth. The Ogopogo had given her nothing but peace, a sense of wonder and belonging. How could they twist its story into something ugly?

She stepped back from the railing, her fists clenched. They didn't understand—none of them did. If this article painted Ogopogo as a killer, it would destroy everything she knew to be true. People would come with fear, with weapons, with no respect for the lake or its guardian.

Maya's jaw tightened with resolve. She had to do something. She had to stop this before it went any further.

"I won't let them ruin you," she whispered under her breath, her gaze fixed on the shimmering water beyond the sprawling yard.

She hurried back into her room, grabbed her backpack, and stuffed her journal inside. Her mind raced. She didn't know Claire Bennett or Emily Fraser personally, but she'd read their work. They were good at what they did—too good. If anyone could reshape the Ogopogo's story, it was them.

Slipping down the back staircase to avoid her parents, Maya darted out the side door and into the evening air. She didn't know exactly how to find them, but she was determined to try.

"They need to hear the truth," she thought, her determination hardening. "And I'm the only one who can tell them."

The lake sparkled in the fading light as Maya set off, her heart pounding with a mix of fear and hope. She didn't know what she'd say when she found Claire and Emily, but one thing was certain, she wouldn't let the Ogopogo's name be dragged through the mud.

Chapter 32

The sun was setting over Ethan's vineyard, casting a golden glow across the neatly lined rows of grapevines. The patio of the rustic stone house overlooked the sprawling Okanagan Valley, and the soft murmur of the lake in the distance completed the idyllic scene. Emily and Liam sat at the long wooden table with Claire and Ethan, glasses of Ethan's finest wine catching the last rays of light.

"This place is incredible," Emily said, looking out at the view. "You've outdone yourself, Ethan."

"Hardly," Ethan replied with a modest smile. "It's the land that does all the work. I'm just here to make sure I don't mess it up."

Claire chuckled, taking a sip of her wine. "You're too humble. Ethan's vineyard has won awards, you know. He's practically the poster boy for Okanagan wine country."

Liam raised his glass in a mock toast. "Here's to being humble and successful. A rare combination."

Ethan laughed, clinking his glass with Liam's. "I'll drink to that."

As the conversation shifted, the topic inevitably returned to the lake, as it often did these days. Emily leaned back in her chair, swirling her wine. "It's hard not to think about the Ogopogo when you're this close to the lake. It's like it has a presence, even when you can't see it."

Claire nodded. "We've been digging into the stories, the sightings, even the history of the lake. But no matter how much research we do, it always feels like there's something just out of reach."

Liam set his glass down, his expression thoughtful. "You know, I've had my own run-in with the lake's mystery."

Emily turned to him, surprised. "You've never mentioned that before."

"It's not exactly something I bring up at dinner parties," Liam said with a grin. "But if we're swapping Ogopogo stories, I might as well share mine."

Ethan leaned back, amused. "Alright, let's hear it. What happened?"

Liam took a moment, as if piecing the memory together. "It was about five years ago. I was out sailing alone, just south of Rattlesnake Island. It was one of those perfect days—clear skies, calm water, not a hint of wind to trouble the sails. I was just drifting, letting the boat glide."

He paused, his eyes narrowing as he relived the moment. "Then, out of nowhere, I saw it. A long, dark shape gliding beneath the surface, maybe fifty feet off the starboard side. It wasn't a wave or a shadow—this thing was moving against the current."

Emily leaned closer, her voice barely above a whisper. "What did it look like?"

Liam shook his head. "That's the thing. It was subtle—just a dark, sinuous form, almost like a shadow. But it was deliberate. It wasn't random movement. It was alive."

Claire's pen was poised over her notebook, her reporter's instincts kicking in. "Did it surface?"

"For a moment," Liam said, nodding. "I saw ridges, like humps, breaking the water. It was there one second and gone the next. I sailed around for another hour, trying to spot it again, but there was nothing. The lake was as calm as ever like it had swallowed whatever it was whole."

Ethan leaned back, his expression thoughtful. "And you're sure it wasn't a log, or fish, or… I don't know, something ordinary?"

Liam gave a wry smile. "I've spent my whole life on that lake. I know the difference between driftwood and something alive. This wasn't ordinary."

Emily glanced at Claire, her eyes sparkling with excitement. "Add that to the growing list of stories. It's amazing how many people have seen something, but there's still no proof."

Ethan refilled his glass, his tone contemplative. "Maybe that's the point. Maybe the lake doesn't want to give up all its secrets."

Claire tapped her notebook, her mind racing. "Or maybe it's waiting for someone to uncover them the right way."

As the group sat under the fading light, the conversation shifted back to lighter topics, but Liam's story lingered in the air like a shadow. The lake, calm and unassuming in the distance, seemed to hold its breath, guarding its mysteries as it always had.

Chapter 33

The early morning light was just beginning to creep over Kelowna when Claire and Emily arrived at the office of the Capital News. The usually bustling downtown streets were eerily quiet, the city still waking from its slumber. Claire fumbled with her keys, balancing a coffee mug in one hand as she was going to unlock the front door.

Emily gasped, nearly spitting out her own coffee. "Claire, look!"

Huddled on the doorstep, wrapped in a thin jacket, was a young girl with light golden blond curls falling over her face. She stirred at the sound of their voices, blinking up at them with wide, tired eyes.

"Maya?" Claire asked, recognizing her from a community event she'd covered a while back. "What are you doing here?"

Maya sat up, rubbing her eyes. "I… I need to talk to Claire Bennett."

Emily crouched down, her voice soft. "Are you okay? Did something happen?"

Maya shook her head, her curls catching the morning light. "No, but I had to come. I couldn't let her print something that isn't true."

Claire and Emily exchanged puzzled looks. "What are you talking about?" Claire asked. "I am Claire Bennett."

Maya stood, clutching her backpack tightly. "The article about the Ogopogo. My dad said you're writing about how it's dangerous, about how it might be responsible for the deaths on the lake. But that's not true! Ogopogo isn't a killer. It's the opposite—it protects the lake."

Emily tilted her head, her curiosity piqued. "What makes you so sure, Maya?"

The girl's eyes filled with a mix of determination and frustration. "Because I've seen it. I've felt it. Ogopogo isn't some monster—it's part of the lake like it's alive. It watches over the water, keeping it safe. People are the ones who don't respect the lake, and that's why bad things happen."

Claire crouched beside Emily, her voice gentle. "Maya, you've seen Ogopogo? Can you tell us more about that?"

Maya hesitated, looking down at her sneakers. "I've seen it a few times. Once, when I was little, it was just a shadow under the water. And again, last year, when I was sitting on the dock. It's big, and it moves like nothing else I've ever seen, but it's not scary. It feels… peaceful."

Emily glanced at Claire, who was scribbling notes in her ever-present notebook. "Why do you think your dad said the article would be about Ogopogo being dangerous?"

Maya's face darkened. "Because he doesn't care about the truth. He only cares about how the lake looks to other people—the tourists, the developers, the ones with money. He thinks the Ogopogo is just a stupid story, but it's not. It's real, and it doesn't deserve to be blamed for things it didn't do."

Claire set her notebook aside and placed a comforting hand on Maya's shoulder. "Maya, I promise you, we're not here to write lies. We're trying to understand the truth about the lake and everything connected to it. If you have something to say, we'll listen."

Maya's eyes filled with tears, but she quickly blinked them away. "I don't care if people don't believe me. I just don't want you to make Ogopogo into something it's not."

Emily smiled softly. "You're brave, Maya. It takes a lot to stand up for what you believe in."

Maya nodded, a spark of determination reigniting in her eyes. "I'll do whatever it takes to protect it. Even if no one else believes me, I know the lake does."

Claire stood, holding out her hand. "How about we get you something warm to drink and talk about this inside? We want to hear your side of the story."

Maya hesitated for a moment before taking Claire's hand. Together, the three of them stepped into the building, the warmth of the newsroom contrasting with the chill of the morning. For the first time in days, Maya felt hope—not just for herself, but for the guardian she knew so well.

Chapter 34

The warm hum of the newsroom enveloped Maya as she sat at the table across from Claire and Emily. A steaming mug of hot chocolate sat in front of her, untouched. Her backpack lay at her feet, its contents spilling slightly—a glimpse of her journal peeking out.

Claire leaned forward, her notebook open. "Maya, you said you've seen Ogopogo. Can you tell us what it looks like?"

Maya hesitated, her fingers playing nervously with the strap of her backpack. Finally, she nodded and reached down, pulling out her worn journal. "I've drawn it," she said softly, placing the journal on the table. "It's easier to show you."

Emily slid the journal closer, carefully flipping through the pages. Each drawing was detailed, vivid, and unmistakably consistent—long, sinuous shapes gliding beneath the water, ridged humps breaking the surface, and soulful eyes that seemed to hold ancient wisdom. The creature came alive on the pages as though Maya had captured its very essence.

"These are incredible," Emily said, her voice barely above a whisper. "You're so talented, Maya."

Claire leaned over to look, her brow furrowing. "Wait a minute…" She flipped back to a particular drawing and then looked at Emily. "These look exactly like Ryan's."

Emily's head shot up, her eyes wide. "You're right. They're almost identical. Maya, have you ever shown these to anyone else? Ryan Stokes, maybe?"

Maya shook her head. "No. I don't even know who Ryan is."

Claire exchanged a knowing glance with Emily. "Ryan. He's an artist—he's been drawing Ogopogo for years. His work has the same details, the ridges, the shape of the head, even the eyes. It's uncanny."

Emily leaned back, her mind racing. "If Maya and Ryan are both drawing the same thing, and they've never met… that means Ryan must have seen Ogopogo too. There's no way this is a coincidence."

Maya tilted her head, her curiosity piqued. "So, this Ryan… he's seen it too? He believes in it?"

Claire nodded. "He believes in it enough to make it the focus of his art. But he's never talked about actually seeing it. He always frames it as inspiration from stories and culture."

Emily tapped her camera. "Or maybe he's kept his sightings to himself, just like Maya has. If they've both seen the same thing and documented it in the same way, that's powerful. It's more than just stories."

Maya's eyes lit up with hope. "Does this mean you believe me?"

Claire smiled warmly. "We believe you, Maya. And I think it's time we talk to Ryan again. If he has more to share, it could change everything."

Maya sat up straighter, a new determination in her voice. "Then I want to come with you. If he's seen Ogopogo, I need to know."

Emily glanced at Claire, a silent agreement passing between them. "Alright," Emily said. "We'll go together. And maybe this time, Ryan will tell us what he's been keeping to himself."

As Maya carefully closed her journal and tucked it back into her bag, the weight of her secret felt a little lighter. For the first time, she wasn't alone in defending the guardian of the lake. Together, they were piecing together a story that was bigger than any of them, a story waiting to be told.

Chapter 35

Maya stood in the quiet hallway of the Capital Newspaper office, clutching her phone tightly in her hand. The morning light filtered through the frosted windows, casting soft patterns on the walls. She took a deep breath and dialed her mom's number, biting her lip as the line rang.

It took a few rings before her mom's bright, distracted voice answered. "Maya, sweetheart! Good morning. Where are you?"

Maya hesitated. "Hi, Mom. I'm… I'm downtown. I am at the newspaper office with Claire Bennett and Emily Fraser."

Her mom paused, clearly processing. "The newspaper office? Claire Bennett? You mean the travel writer?"

"Yeah, her," Maya said, her voice steady. "I… I wanted to talk to her and Emily about something important. About Ogopogo."

There was a brief silence, then a light laugh. "Maya, you and that lake creature. You're obsessed. What's going on, honey? Did something happen?"

Maya's grip tightened on the phone. "Mom, it's not just stories. I've seen it. And Claire and Emily are trying to write about Ogopogo, but they don't understand it. I need to help them, and they're taking me to meet a man who draws Ogopogo—just like I do."

Her mom's voice softened, the distraction fading slightly. "Maya… you know I love that you're creative, but are you sure these people aren't just humoring you?"

"No, Mom!" Maya's voice rose slightly, and she quickly lowered it, glancing back at the newsroom where Claire and Emily were waiting. "They believe me. Claire said my drawings look just like his. How could that happen if Ogopogo wasn't real?"

Her mom sighed, the sound tinged with resignation. "Claire Bennett… I know her a little. She came to one of our parties a while back. She seemed nice. And Emily Fraser, isn't she the photographer?"

"Yeah," Maya said quickly. "They're good people, Mom. They just want to know the truth, and so do I."

Another pause, and then her mom's tone shifted to something lighter, almost amused. "Alright, sweetheart. If Claire's involved, I trust her to look out for you. But you need to promise me you'll keep your phone on and call me if anything happens."

Maya felt a surge of relief. "I promise. Thank you, Mom."

"Just… don't go jumping into the lake or anything crazy," her mom said with a laugh. "And let me know when you're coming home. I'll have Pierre make something special for dinner."

Maya smiled. "Okay, I will. Thanks, Mom. Love you."

"Love you too, honey. Be careful."

As the call ended, Maya slipped the phone back into her pocket and took a deep breath. She turned and walked back into the newsroom, where Claire and Emily were waiting by the door.

"Well?" Claire asked, her expression curious.

"She said yes," Maya replied with a small smile. "She knows you, Claire. She trusts you."

Claire chuckled. "Good to know I have a decent reputation."

Emily grinned, slinging her camera bag over her shoulder. "Alright, let's go meet Ryan. Something tells me this is going to be an interesting conversation."

Maya followed them out the door, her heart lighter but her resolve stronger than ever. She didn't know what Ryan would say or if it would bring her closer to protecting the Ogopogo, but she was ready to find out.

Chapter 36

The wooden door of the art studio creaked open as Claire stepped inside, a smile playing on her lips. The room smelled of oil paint and cedar, with shelves of neatly arranged brushes and paints lining the walls. The morning light filtered through the large windows, illuminating several unfinished canvases propped against the walls.

"Mr. Stokes," Claire called, her tone teasing. "I think you've been holding out on us."

Ryan appeared from behind an easel, wiping his hands on a paint-smeared cloth. His dark eyes narrowed in mock suspicion. "Claire, always with the dramatics. What am I accused of now?"

Claire smirked and gestured to Maya, who stood hesitantly in the doorway, clutching her journal. "This is Maya. She has something you need to see."

Ryan's gaze softened as he looked at Maya. "Well, come in, Maya. I don't bite."

Maya stepped forward, holding her journal tightly to her chest. "Hi, Mr. Stokes. Claire said you draw Ogopogo, too?"

Ryan raised an eyebrow and glanced at Claire, who nodded encouragingly. "She's telling the truth," Claire said. "Maya's drawings look just like yours. It's uncanny."

Ryan leaned against his workbench, intrigued. "Let's see them, then."

Maya hesitated, then slowly opened her journal and handed it to him. Ryan flipped through the pages, his expression shifting from curiosity to awe. He paused on a particularly detailed sketch of Ogopogo, its ridged back breaking the water's surface, its eyes soulful and watchful.

"These are remarkable," Ryan said softly, looking up at Maya. "You've captured the essence of something ancient, something… alive."

Maya's eyes lit up. "You think so? Claire said our drawings are the same."

Ryan walked over to a large canvas and pulled it into view. It was a striking image of Ogopogo, painted in deep blues and greens, with golden highlights tracing its ridges. The creature seemed to emerge from the canvas, both majestic and mysterious.

Maya gasped. "It's just like mine!"

Claire crossed her arms, her voice filled with knowing. "So, Ryan, care to explain how you and Maya are drawing the same creature?"

Ryan hesitated, his gaze flickering between the women and Maya. Finally, he sighed. "I wasn't going to say anything because… well, it's hard to explain. But yes, I've seen it."

Emily leaned forward, her voice sharp with excitement. "You've seen Ogopogo? When?"

"Years ago," Ryan said, his tone serious. "I was kayaking near Rattlesnake Island. It was late afternoon, and the water was calm. At first, I thought it was just a shadow, but then it moved—smooth and deliberate. I saw the ridges on its back, the way it glided just below the surface. It wasn't like anything I'd ever seen before."

Claire's pen flew across her notebook as she asked, "Why didn't you tell anyone?"

Ryan chuckled dryly, shaking his head. "Can you imagine the headlines? 'Local Artist Claims to See Lake Monster.' It would've made me a laughingstock. So, I kept it to myself and let my art do the talking."

Maya stepped closer to the canvas, her voice barely above a whisper. "You believe it's real, don't you?"

Ryan nodded. "I do. And now, seeing your drawings, I know I'm not the only one who's seen it."

Claire looked at him, her expression a mix of frustration and admiration. "You've been holding back, Ryan. This could change everything."

Ryan gave her a small smile. "Maybe it's time for the story to come out. But if we're going to do this, we need to do it right. The Ogopogo isn't just a creature—it's a symbol, a guardian. People need to see it for what it truly is."

Emily snapped a photo of the canvas, her excitement barely contained. "This is incredible. Between Maya's story and your experience, we're starting to get a clearer picture of what's out there."

Maya beamed, her heart swelling with pride. For the first time, she felt like she wasn't alone in her connection to the lake and its guardian.

As the group stood in Ryan's studio, the pieces of the puzzle began to fall into place. Ogopogo wasn't just a legend or a myth—it was a living, breathing part of the lake, waiting for its story to be told.

Chapter 37

Ryan stood, pacing the studio as he spoke. The weight of the stories he carried seemed to fill the room, and the women listened intently as he began to weave the tales that had shaped his understanding of nx̌ax̌aitkʷ.

"My grandfather's grandfather told about the old ways," Ryan began, his voice carrying the cadence of oral tradition. "Before the settlers, before the towns, the Syilx people knew the lake was alive. They called it nx̌ax̌aitkʷ, not because they feared it, but because they respected its power."

He paused, running a hand over the rough edge of a wooden carving resting on his workbench. "One story my grandfather loved to tell was about the salmon runs. The people depended on the salmon to survive, but they also knew they had to leave enough for the lake. One year, the run was thin, and some of the younger men took more than they should have. They ignored the elders' warnings. The next day, the men went out to fish again, but the lake had turned against them. Their nets tore, their boats capsized, and they swore they saw something massive gliding beneath them, watching."

Maya's eyes were wide as she listened. "Did they ever catch anything after that?"

Ryan smiled faintly. "The elders performed a ceremony, making an offering of the first fish caught. They asked nx̌ax̌aitkʷ for forgiveness. Only then did the salmon return. It wasn't about punishment—it was about restoring balance."

Claire tapped her pen against her notebook. "So, it's not just about the lake's resources. It's about the relationship between people and the land."

"Exactly," Ryan said. "Another story my grandfather told was about the island—Rattlesnake Island, as it's called now. He said it wasn't always just an island. It was a place where the spirit rested, a sanctuary within the lake. People didn't go there unless they were invited, in dreams or visions. To disturb it was to disturb the lake's peace."

Emily frowned. "But now it's a tourist attraction. People go there all the time."

Ryan nodded, his expression darkening. "And the lake has changed because of it. My grandfather believed that the more we disrupt the balance, the more we'll see nx̌ax̌aitkʷ. Not as a guardian, but as a warning."

Maya clutched her journal tighter. "That's why people see it more now. It's not trying to hurt anyone—it's trying to protect the lake."

Ryan turned to her, his gaze thoughtful. "You might be right, Maya. It's rare for someone as young as you to feel that connection, but you do. That means something."

Claire shifted in her seat, her brow furrowed. "But if it's trying to protect the lake, why don't more people understand? Why are there still stories of it being dangerous?"

Ryan sighed, leaning against his workbench. "Because people fear what they don't understand. They see something big, something they can't explain, and their first instinct is to call it a monster. It's easier than admitting that maybe the lake isn't ours to control."

Emily glanced at the canvas of Ogopogo on the easel. "Have you ever gone back to Rattlesnake Island, Ryan? Since you saw it?"

Ryan hesitated, his fingers brushing against the carving on the bench. "No. The first time I saw nx̌ax̌aitkʷ was near the island. It felt… sacred. Like I was intruding. I haven't been back because I don't think it was meant for me to see again. The lake shows itself when it needs to, not when we want it to."

Maya stood, her golden curls catching the light. "I want to go there. I need to see it again. Maybe if people could understand it like we do, they'd stop treating it like a monster."

Claire exchanged a glance with Emily, her pen pausing over her notebook. "That's a big step, Maya. But maybe she's right. Maybe the only way to tell this story is to go to the heart of it."

Ryan crossed his arms, his gaze serious. "If you go, you need to be prepared. The lake doesn't give up its secrets easily. And nx̌ax̌aitkʷ… it doesn't just appear for anyone."

Maya's voice was firm, her determination shining through. "It will for me. I know it will."

The room fell silent, the weight of her words lingering in the air. The lake, calm and mysterious in the distance, seemed to call to them all its secrets waiting to be uncovered.

Chapter 38

The boat hummed steadily as it cut through the calm waters of Okanagan Lake, the morning sun casting golden rays across the surface. Liam stood at the helm, steering the boat toward Rattlesnake Island. Claire, Emily, and Maya sat in the back, the wind tousling their hair. Maya clutched her journal, her excitement barely contained.

"You've been out here before, Liam?" Emily asked, adjusting her camera strap.

"A few times," Liam said, keeping his eyes on the horizon. "Mostly for sailing, but I've anchored near the island once or twice. It's a strange place—quiet, almost too quiet. You'll see."

Maya leaned over the edge of the boat, her golden curls glinting in the sunlight. "Do you think we'll see it? Ogopogo?"

Claire placed a reassuring hand on her shoulder. "We're here to find answers, Maya. Whatever happens, we'll respect the lake and its guardian."

As the boat neared the island, the group fell silent. Rattlesnake Island loomed ahead, its rocky shoreline steeped in a mysterious stillness. Liam slowed the boat and eased it toward a small cove.

"Here we are," he said, cutting the engine. "Welcome to Rattlesnake Island."

They stepped onto the shore, the crunch of gravel beneath their feet breaking the eerie quiet. The island felt untouched, as though time had forgotten it. Maya's gaze darted around, her eyes wide with wonder.

"This place is amazing," Emily murmured, her camera clicking as she captured the rugged beauty of the island.

As they ventured inland, they stumbled upon the remnants of what appeared to be a mini-golf course. Rusted poles jutted from the ground, and faded patches of artificial turf lay hidden beneath overgrown weeds.

Claire crouched down, brushing away debris. "This must be what's left of that failed amusement park. I read about it—someone tried to turn the island into a tourist attraction decades ago, but it never took off."

Liam shook his head, his voice low. "It feels out of place. Like it doesn't belong here."

Maya wandered toward the shoreline, drawn to the gentle lapping of the water. She slipped off her sandals and waded in, the cool lake water rippling around her ankles.

"Be careful, Maya," Claire called, watching her from the edge.

Maya turned back, a serene smile on her face. "It's okay. I feel safe here."

Before anyone could respond, the water around Maya began to stir. Ripples spread outward, breaking the stillness of the lake. The group froze, their eyes fixed on the shimmering surface.

And then, it appeared.

A long, sinuous shape glided just beneath the water, its ridged back breaking the surface for a fleeting moment. The sunlight caught the creature's form, highlighting its sleek, dark body and the graceful way it moved.

"Is that—" Emily started, his voice barely a whisper.

"I believe so," Claire said, her tone a mix of awe and disbelief.

Maya stood perfectly still, the water swirling around her knees. The creature swam closer, its movements deliberate and calm. It ridges glistening in the sunlight, before disappearing into the depths with a final flick of its tail.

Emily's camera hung forgotten around her neck, her hands trembling. "Did… did that just happen?"

"It did," Claire said, her voice filled with wonder.

Maya turned back to them, her golden curls wet and clinging to her cheeks. Her smile was radiant. "It's not a monster. It's beautiful."

Liam ran a hand through his hair, shaking his head in disbelief. "It is just like what I thought I saw years ago."

Claire placed a hand on his shoulder, her eyes still fixed on the water. "We're witnesses now too. This changes everything."

Emily finally raised her camera, snapping a photo of the water where the creature had disappeared. "No one's going to believe this."

Maya stepped out of the water, her face glowing with excitement. "They don't have to. Ogopogo doesn't need people to believe in it. It knows what it is."

As they stood together on the shoreline, the weight of what they had just seen began to sink in. The lake, the island, the guardian— they were part of something far greater than they could have imagined.

Chapter 39

Claire and Emily sat across from each other in their favorite corner of the cafe, the aroma of fresh pastries and coffee enveloping the cozy space. Their notebooks and laptops were spread out between them, along with Maya's journal and a few photos Emily had snapped on Rattlesnake Island. The weight of their recent encounter with Ogopogo hung in the air.

Emily stirred her latte absently. "So, how do we even begin to write this? We've got folklore, real-life sightings, cultural significance, and now our own experience. It's not just a story—it's… everything."

Claire leaned back in her chair, staring at her notes. "That's the challenge. It can't just be another article about a lake monster. It has to mean something. We have to respect the Syilx stories, the science, and the eyewitness accounts while also acknowledging what we've seen."

Emily nodded. "Ryan's perspective and Maya's drawings add so much, but I don't want it to come across as sensationalized. If we focus too much on the mystery, we risk losing the heart of what Ogopogo represents."

"Agreed," Claire said. "It's not about proving it exists—it's about showing people that the lake and its guardian are part of something much bigger. The connection to the land, the respect for balance—it's all tied together."

Emily tapped her camera. "What about the title? Something that captures the essence of the piece without making it sound like a tabloid."

Claire thought for a moment, then smiled. "How about 'Guardian of the Lake: The Stories and Spirit of Ogopogo'? It hints at the mystery while focusing on the deeper meaning."

Emily grinned. "I like it. It's respectful and intriguing without being over the top. Now, how do we structure it?"

Claire flipped to a fresh page in her notebook, jotting down ideas. "We start with the cultural roots—the Syilx stories about nx̌ax̌aitkʷ and what it represents. Then we bring in the science—what we know about the lake, its history, and phenomena like seiches."

"And then?" Emily asked.

"Eyewitness accounts," Claire said, her pen moving quickly. "We include Ryan's story, Maya's drawings, and maybe even Liam's experience. We frame it all as a mosaic of perspectives, showing how Ogopogo is more than just a creature—it's a symbol."

Emily nodded, her excitement growing. "I can add the photos I took—Rattlesnake Island, Ryan's art, Maya's journal. They'll bring the story to life."

Claire looked up from her notes, her expression serious. "We'll also need to address the deaths on the lake. Not in a way that blames Ogopogo, but to explore the idea of balance and respect. The lake is powerful—it demands caution."

Emily sipped her latte thoughtfully. "And we finish with what we saw. Not as proof but as our own piece of the puzzle. We can't ignore it, but we don't have to shout it from the rooftops either."

Claire smiled. "Exactly. The story isn't about convincing anyone. It's about sharing the layers of meaning behind Ogopogo and letting people decide for themselves."

Emily leaned back, a sense of relief washing over her. "This could be our best piece yet."

Claire nodded, her determination shining through. "And the most important. Let's make sure we get it right."

As they settled into their work, the bakery around them buzzed with life, but their focus remained sharp. They weren't just writing an article—they were crafting a narrative that honored the lake, its guardian, and the stories that had shaped the region for generations.

Chapter 40

Ellie sat at her desk in the rented workspace she had converted into a makeshift lab, a cup of lukewarm coffee in her hand. Papers, notes, and charts about Okanagan Lake were scattered across every surface, a testament to her relentless pursuit of answers. The knock on the door startled her from her thoughts.

"Come in," she called, setting down her coffee.

Claire and Emily entered their expressions, a mix of excitement and apprehension. Claire carried her notebook under one arm while Emily had her camera slung over her shoulder, as always.

"Hey, Ellie," Claire said, trying to gauge her mood. "We need to talk."

Ellie arched an eyebrow. "That tone usually means something happened."

Emily nodded, unable to hide the smile tugging at her lips. "You're not going to believe this, Ellie. We saw it."

Ellie froze, her eyes narrowing. "Saw what?"

"Ogopogo," Claire said, her voice barely above a whisper. "We were on Rattlesnake Island with Liam and Maya. It swam right by her."

Ellie blinked, processing their words. "Wait. You saw it? Like, actually saw it? And you didn't think to invite me?"

Emily winced. "It wasn't exactly planned. Liam offered to take us out there, and it just… happened."

Ellie stood, crossing her arms. "Happened? You saw what I've been studying for months—what I've been chasing for years—and it just happened?"

Claire stepped forward, her voice soft. "Ellie, we're sorry. We didn't know it would show itself. It was incredible, but we weren't trying to leave you out."

Ellie paced the room, frustration written all over her face. "Do you have any idea how much this research means to me? I've been trying to prove something like this exists my entire career. And now, when I'm running out of time and funding, you two stumble onto the one thing I've been searching for?"

Emily hesitated. "Ellie, we have photos. I didn't get a clear shot of the creature, but I captured the ripples and the moment after it disappeared. It's something."

Ellie stopped pacing, her shoulders slumping slightly. "Something. I guess that's better than nothing."

Claire set her notebook on the desk. "Look, we know this is hard for you. But you're still a part of this. We couldn't make sense of what we saw without your work and expertise. You've been the one grounding us in science while we've been chasing stories."

Ellie sighed, running a hand through her braid. "It's not just that. My funding is running out. I've got maybe a week left before I have to pack up and leave. I thought I'd have more time, but grants don't come easily for research like this."

Emily and Claire exchanged a glance, their excitement dampened by Ellie's words.

"We'll figure something out," Emily said, her tone firm. "This can't be the end of your research. Maybe the article can help drum up interest or support."

Ellie gave a small, humorless laugh. "You think an article will get people to take this seriously? They'll just think it's another lake monster story, another piece of sensationalism."

Claire shook her head. "Not the way we're writing it. It's about the lake, the spirit, the history. It's about more than just proving Ogopogo exists. It's about why it matters."

Ellie looked at them, her frustration giving way to a flicker of hope. "You really believe people will care?"

Emily smiled. "We care, Ellie. And if we care, others will too."

Ellie sighed, her resolve softening. "Alright. Show me what you've got. If I'm going to run out of time, I might as well go out swinging."

Claire opened her notebook, and Emily retrieved her camera, ready to share their findings. As they dove into their stories and evidence, Ellie's frustration began to fade, replaced by a renewed determination. She wasn't ready to give up—not yet.

Chapter 41

Ellie sat at the table with Claire and Emily, flipping through the photos Emily had captured on Rattlesnake Island. Her eyes lingered on the ripples in the water, imagining the faint traces of something just beneath the surface.

"It's not definitive," she said, her voice tinged with frustration. "But it's… compelling."

Emily leaned forward. "It's more than that, Ellie. It's part of a bigger picture. Your research, Ryan's stories, Maya's drawings—it all fits together."

Claire tapped her pen against her notebook. "We can use this, Ellie. Not just for the article but to raise awareness. Maybe even to secure more funding for your work."

Ellie leaned back, crossing her arms. "You really think one article is going to convince people to take this seriously? I'm a scientist, Claire. I need data, evidence, something tangible. Not folklore and shadows."

Claire nodded. "I get that, but think about it. If people read this and start seeing the lake differently—not as a tourist spot but as something sacred, something worth protecting—that's a start. And maybe it brings in the kind of attention that could lead to more support for you."

Ellie looked at her skeptically. "You think an article can do all that?"

Emily smiled. "It's not just an article, Ellie. It's a story. And stories have power. They make people feel something. They make them care."

Ellie sighed, her fingers drumming on the table. "Alright. Let's say you're right. What's the next step?"

"We need more," Claire said firmly. "More stories, more evidence. Something concrete to tie everything together. The lake, the spirit, the creature—it's all connected, but we need to show that connection."

Emily glanced at her camera. "Maybe we go back to the island. Spend more time there. If Ogopogo showed itself once, maybe it will again."

Ellie frowned. "It's not that simple. If the stories are true, it doesn't appear on demand. It shows itself when it needs to, not because we want it to."

Maya, who had been sitting quietly nearby, spoke up. "Maybe it will show itself again if we show respect. Ryan said the lake responds to how we treat it, right?"

Claire turned to her, intrigued. "What are you suggesting?"

Maya hesitated, then said, "An offering. Like Ryan talked about. Not just to see it again, but to show we're here for the right reasons."

Ellie's eyebrows shot up. "You want to perform a ceremony?"

Maya nodded, her golden curls bouncing with the motion. "It's not just about seeing Ogopogo. It's about showing it we understand."

Emily smiled at her. "I like it. It's respectful, and it might give us a deeper connection to the lake."

Claire looked at Ellie. "What do you think?"

Ellie hesitated, then sighed. "It's not exactly scientific, but… it can't hurt. If nothing else, it'll give us insight into the cultural practices tied to the lake."

Claire grinned. "Then it's settled. We'll talk to Ryan, figure out what kind of offering is appropriate, and head back to the island."

As they finalized their plans, a renewed sense of purpose filled the room. The lake had its secrets, and they were determined to uncover them—not to exploit them, but to understand and protect them.

Ellie glanced at the photos again, her resolve hardening. "Alright, let's do this. If we're going to tell this story, we're going to do it right."

Chapter 42

The soft light of early evening bathed the lake in hues of gold and lavender as the group gathered on the rocky shores of Rattlesnake Island. The calm water stretched endlessly, reflecting the fading light like a mirror. Ryan stood at the edge of the shore, his presence commanding yet serene, as he arranged the offerings with careful precision.

Maya watched intently, clutching her journal close to her chest. Claire and Emily stood nearby, their notebooks and cameras ready but tucked away for now out of respect for the moment. Ellie shifted uncomfortably, her scientific mind grappling with the significance of the ritual. Liam and Ethan exchanged quiet words, their eyes scanning the horizon as if expecting the lake to respond at any moment.

Ryan turned to the group, his voice low and steady. "This isn't about calling nx̌ax̌aitkʷ to us. It's about showing gratitude—for the lake, its gifts, and the balance it keeps. The offering is a symbol of our respect."

He knelt, placing a bundle of cedar branches, sweetgrass, and a small pouch of tobacco at the water's edge. "These are traditional offerings. The cedar for cleansing, the sweetgrass for connection, and the tobacco for our prayers."

Ryan motioned for Maya to step forward. She hesitated, then knelt beside him, her golden curls catching the last rays of sunlight. "Maya," he said softly, "You've felt the lake's spirit more than any of us. You should place the offering."

Maya nodded, her hands trembling slightly as she took the pouch of tobacco. She whispered something under her breath—a silent prayer or perhaps a message meant only for the lake—and gently placed the pouch on the water. The waves lapped at her offering, carrying it slowly away.

Ryan stood and raised his hands. "Now, we wait. Not for something to happen, but for the lake to hear us."

The group fell silent. The only sounds were the gentle rustling of the wind and the rhythmic lapping of the water against the shore. Minutes passed, stretching into what felt like hours. The tension in the air was palpable. Each person lost in their thoughts.

Ellie's scientific curiosity finally broke the silence. "Ryan," she said quietly, "Do you really think the lake will respond?"

Ryan turned to her, his expression calm but serious. "It's not about what I think. It's about what the lake chooses to show us. Nx̌ax̌aitkʷ doesn't appear for spectacle. It appears for balance."

Suddenly, the water near the shore rippled unnaturally, breaking the calm surface. Maya gasped, stepping back instinctively. The group froze, their eyes locked on the water.

The ripples grew larger, spreading outward in perfect, rhythmic patterns. And then, slowly, a long, dark shape emerged just beneath the surface. The ridges along its back glinted in the fading light, and for a fleeting moment, the group saw the unmistakable form of Ogopogo. It glided gracefully, its movements deliberate and powerful, before disappearing into the depths once more.

Maya's face lit up with wonder. "It heard us," she whispered, her voice trembling with awe.

Emily fumbled with her camera but stopped herself, letting the moment pass without interruption. Claire placed a hand on her shoulder, both women too moved to speak.

Ellie stared at the water, her logical mind struggling to process what she had just witnessed. "I… I don't even know how to explain that," she admitted, her voice hushed.

Ryan smiled faintly. "Some things aren't meant to be explained. They're meant to be understood."

Liam and Ethan exchanged a glance, their disbelief replaced by quiet reverence. "I've never seen anything like that," Ethan said, his voice barely above a whisper.

As the sun dipped below the horizon, the group stood together in silence, the weight of the moment settling over them. The lake, once mysterious and unknowable, had revealed a piece of itself—just enough to remind them of its power, its presence, and its balance.

Ryan finally broke the silence. "Let's leave it here. The lake has given us what we came for."

They began their journey back to the boat, each carrying the experience in their own way. For Maya, it was a confirmation of what she had always believed. For Ellie, it was a challenge to her understanding of the natural world. And for Claire and Emily, it was the heart of a story that had to be told with care and reverence.

Chapter 43

The Article

Headline:
Guardian of the Lake: The Stories, Spirit, and Mystery of Ogopogo
By Claire Bennett and Emily Fraser

Introduction
Okanagan Lake, with its sprawling waters and breathtaking views, is a cherished landmark of British Columbia. It is a place of recreation, inspiration, and mystery. For generations, it has also been home to one of the most enduring legends of the Pacific Northwest: Ogopogo, or as the Syilx people call it, nx̌ax̌aitkʷ.

Often dismissed as folklore or relegated to the realm of tourism gimmicks, Ogopogo is far more than a mythical lake monster. It is a symbol of balance, a guardian of the lake, and a connection to the deep history of the land and its people.

The Cultural Roots

For the Syilx people, nx̌ax̌aitkʷ is not just a creature but a sacred spirit of the lake. Oral traditions describe it as a protector, embodying the essence of Okanagan Lake itself. Offerings of cedar, sweetgrass, and tobacco have been made for generations to honor its presence and ensure harmony between the people and the lake.

Ryan Stokes, a Syilx artist, shared stories passed down through his family, including accounts of the lake turning against those who disrespected its waters. "It's about balance," he explained. "The lake gives us life, but it demands respect. Nx̌ax̌aitkʷ reminds us of that balance."

Accompanying Image

A vibrant painting by Ryan Stokes depicting nx̌ax̌aitkʷ gliding gracefully through the water. The creature's ridged back, and soulful eyes are rendered with intricate detail, set against the shimmering blues and greens of the lake.

Science Meets Myth

Okanagan Lake is one of the deepest in British Columbia, carved by glaciers over thousands of years. Its depths are shrouded in mystery, with reports of underwater caves and standing waves known as seiches. While these phenomena explain some of the lake's oddities, they do not account for the countless sightings of a large, serpentine creature.

Dr. Ellie Marston, a marine biologist, has spent months studying the lake. "What we're seeing isn't just myth," she said. "There are patterns—sightings concentrated in certain areas, ripples that defy explanation, and shadows that move against the current. The lake holds secrets we're only beginning to understand."

Accompanying Image

A map of Okanagan Lake, highlighting key locations of sightings and areas of geological interest, including Rattlesnake Island and City Park.

Eyewitness Accounts

Eyewitness stories breathe life into the legend of Ogopogo. Among them are the vivid recollections of Ryan Stokes, who saw the creature while kayaking near Rattlesnake Island, and Maya Lawrence, a young girl whose drawings of Ogopogo mirror Ryan's art despite the two having never met.

"I wasn't scared," Maya said. "It felt like it was watching over me like it knew I understood it wasn't a monster."

Accompanying Image

Maya's journal open to a page filled with detailed sketches of Ogopogo, its ridged back and flowing body eerily similar to Ryan's depiction.

A Moment of Connection

During a recent visit to Rattlesnake Island, our team witnessed something extraordinary. After participating in a traditional offering led by Ryan Stokes, the water stirred in an unmistakable way. A long, dark shape glided beneath the surface, its ridged back briefly breaking the calm water before vanishing.

We stood in awe, humbled by the lake's response to the ritual. Whether this was the elusive nx̌ax̌aitkʷ or a natural phenomenon, it reminded us of the lake's profound mystery and power.

Accompanying Image

A photo of the lake at sunset, the water rippling in the spot where Ogopogo had appeared. The golden hues of the sky reflect the reverence of the moment.

The Truth of the Lake

Ogopogo's story is not one of fear or danger

but of connection. It represents the lake's soul, a guardian reminding us to honor and protect the water and the life it sustains. Whether you believe in the creature itself, its message is universal: balance, respect, and coexistence.

Accompanying Image

The group standing together on the shores of Rattlesnake Island silhouetted against the shimmering lake, a testament to the bond they now share with the legend and spirit of the lake.

Conclusion

Okanagan Lake's mysteries run deep, and its stories weave together culture, nature, and the human spirit. Whether nx̌ax̌aitkʷ is real or symbolic, its presence resonates with those who take the time to listen. It's not just about what you see on the surface—it's about what you feel in the depths.

Chapter 44

The article hit the newsstands and online platforms early in the morning, and by midday, the Kelowna Capital Newspaper's phones were ringing off the hook. Social media buzzed with reactions as readers from across the Okanagan Valley—and beyond— shared their thoughts on *Guardian of the Lake: The Stories, Spirit, and Mystery of Ogopogo.*

At the cafe, Claire and Emily sat at their usual table, laptops open as they monitored the flood of comments and emails pouring in. Maya was with them, nervously stirring a hot chocolate as she read over Claire's shoulder.

"This is incredible," Emily said, scrolling through the Capital Newspaper's Instagram feed. "People are sharing their own stories— sightings, encounters, and even family legends about Ogopogo. Look at this one."

She turned her laptop toward Claire, showing a comment from a man in Vernon: *My grandfather always swore he saw Ogopogo near Rattlesnake Island when he was a boy. Thank you for treating this story with the respect it deserves.*

Claire smiled, her fingers flying over her keyboard as she replied. "I'm seeing so many similar comments. People seem relieved that we didn't sensationalize it. They're proud of the cultural focus."

Maya leaned closer, her golden curls brushing Claire's arm. "What about the mean comments? Are there any of those?"

Claire paused, then gave Maya a reassuring smile. "Of course, there are a few skeptics. But they're mostly asking questions, not attacking. And that's okay. It means we've got people thinking."

Emily grinned. "You mean this one? 'It's just a big fish. Get over it.' Honestly, I'll take that over some of the stuff I've seen online."

Maya giggled, her nervousness easing. "At least they're reading it."

Across the valley, the article sparked conversations in coffee shops, schools, and dinner tables. At a local bookstore, a group of retirees gathered to discuss the cultural significance of Ogopogo. At the university, students in an environmental studies class debated the ecological aspects of the lake and its potential guardianship.

Even Ryan was feeling the ripple effect. His studio phone rang constantly with requests for interviews and offers to showcase his art. He had sold two prints of his Ogopogo painting within hours of the article's release.

At the Newspaper's office, the editor asked Ellie to stop by. Holding a printed copy of the article. "This piece is phenomenal," he said, his tone brimming with pride. "We've had record traffic on the site today. And Ellie, your scientific input has gotten some serious attention. I've already had a couple of researchers ask if you're available for collaboration."

Ellie, who had been half-heartedly thinking about packing up her equipment, paused mid-motion. "Seriously?"

"Seriously," he said with a grin. "Looks like you're not done with the lake just yet."

Ellie's face lit up with hope as she glanced at the article. "Maybe there's still time to figure out what's really going on down there."

By evening, the article had gone viral, reigniting a fascination that many had thought was fading. Major outlets across Canada and beyond picked it up, sparking debates, discussions, and excitement. National Geographic, which had covered Ogopogo in a short feature years ago, tweeted a link to the Kelowna Capital's article with the caption:

Guardian of the Lake: A deep dive into the cultural, scientific, and spiritual mystery of Ogopogo. Could this be Canada's Nessie—finally understood?

The tweet referenced their past coverage, acknowledging how the Kelowna Capital's Newspaper fresh perspective brought depth and humanity to the story. Comments flooded in beneath the post, with readers sharing their own encounters, tagging friends, and debating the existence of Ogopogo.

This new wave of interest was built on decades of curiosity but took it further—no longer just asking if Ogopogo existed but questioning what it truly represented for the people of the Okanagan Valley and beyond.

Meanwhile, local businesses capitalized on the buzz. A bakery in Vernon created Ogopogo Donuts shaped like the serpent, while a Kelowna brewery announced a new Guardian Lager in honor of the lake's mysterious protector.

At home that night, Claire scrolled through the flood of emails, a satisfied smile on her face. One in particular caught her attention. It was from an environmental organization in Vancouver, offering to fund a public awareness campaign to preserve Okanagan Lake.

"This is bigger than we thought," she said to Emily, who was lounging on the couch with a glass of wine.

Emily nodded. "It's not just about Ogopogo. It's about the lake, the land, the stories. People are finally paying attention."

Claire's phone buzzed. It was Maya.

"Hi, sweetheart," Claire answered softly.

"Claire... do you think Ogopogo knows what we're doing?"

Claire paused, her eyes drifting to the lake outside, calm and luminous.

"I think the lake knows," she said gently. "And I think... Ogopogo has always known."

Maya was silent for a moment, then whispered, "Tell it we're sorry it had to wait so long."

Claire smiled, tears in her eyes. "We just did."

Outside, a soft wind stirred the surface of the lake, and for a moment, it rippled—not with waves, but with memory.

And deep beneath, where ancient waters held the echoes of time and story, something stirred in gratitude.

The Okanagan had not just rediscovered its guardian.

It had remembered its soul.

Poems

Ogopogo Song

Down in the depths where the water flows,
By Okanagan Lake, where the mystery grows,
Legends speak of a creature below,
O-G-O-P-O-G-O!

O-G-O-P-O-G-O,
He is the biggest fish I know!
Swimming deep where the currents go,
O-G-O-P-O-G-O!

Some say he's shy, some say he's bold,
A story passed down from the days of old.
When the moonlight shines, and the waters glow,
You might just see O-G-O-P-O-G-O!

O-G-O-P-O-G-O,
He is the biggest fish I know!
Swimming deep where the currents go,
O-G-O-P-O-G-O!

Is he real, or just a tale?
A shadow that glides with the breeze or the

sail?
We watch and we wait, but only he knows,
The secret of O-G-O-P-O-G-O!

O-G-O-P-O-G-O,
He is the biggest fish I know!
Swimming deep where the currents go,
O-G-O-P-O-G-O!

So come to the lake, where the waters gleam,
Search for the monster of legend and dream.
With a splash or a wave, he might just show,
O-G-O-P-O-G-O!

Frank Brummet *(my father-in-law)*

Nick (hubby) and I were discussing this book when he
remembered a time when he was about five, his dad
was playing the guitar and singing him and his three
other siblings this song…(or a version of it anyways).
Frank was talented like that, making up lyrics and
poems.

The Countries I Love

In that beautiful country way over the sea,
Where to school I toddled when only three.
My memory is clear of the songs that we
sang,
And the games that we played, in that fair
land.

Oh garden of England, fair country of
Kent,
Where the greater part of my childhood I
spent.
Those cherished memories so dear to my
heart,
Meadows of cowslips, the song of the lark.

Red poppies in wheat fields, cornflowers of
blue,
Dainty white Margarets and buttercups too.
Picnics in the woods gathering chestnuts to
eat,
Yes, those days in the country, they were
such a treat.

Watching fruit being harvested, there were
apples galore.
Hops roasting in kilns, then to market for
sure.
Beloved grandparents, living just up the

street,
Often I knocked on their door for a hug
and a treat.

We shopped often at Maidstone just a few
miles away,
Then lazily, watching the boats on the
winding Medway.
But oh, sad, sad day, when leaving loved
ones behind,
We sailed the deep ocean our fortunes to
find.

Our journey at last ended in Okanagan
Valley fair.
How lucky we were in making our home
here.
For so many years I have enjoyed this lovely
valley,
This blessed spot, the Okanagan Valley.

Jessie B. Fletcher *(my paternal grandmother)*

She was born in Islington, County of Kent, England
and moved to the Okanagan when she was eight years
old.

Acknowledgments

Writing *Guardian of the Lake* has been a journey of creativity, reflection, and deep appreciation for the people and places that made this story possible.

First and foremost, I want to express my heartfelt gratitude to my family for their unwavering love, patience, and belief in me. Growing up in the Okanagan, I was surrounded by its quiet beauty, and your support gave me the freedom to revisit those cherished landscapes and explore the themes of mystery, heritage, and healing that shape this novel.

A special thank you to the Okanagan Valley—its breathtaking landscapes, shimmering lake views, rugged cedar groves, and vibrant communities provided both the backdrop and heartbeat of this story. The region's rich history, enduring legends, and timeless charm inspired every word, every scene, and every thread of connection woven into this tale.

To the Syilx Okanagan heritage and stories, I offer my deepest respect and gratitude. Your enduring connection to the land, water, and traditions influenced the soul of this novel and reminded me of the importance of honoring the past while moving forward with care and intention.

To my mentors, colleagues, and fellow writers—thank you for your encouragement, insight, and thoughtful feedback. Your guidance helped me shape this story with authenticity and depth.

To my readers, thank you for stepping into the world of Guardian of the Lake. It is my hope that this story resonates with your hearts, inspires reflection, and reminds you of the beauty found in resilience, connection, and the courage to embrace the unknown.

Finally, I extend my gratitude to the creative spirit that continues to guide my writing and to the timeless stories of the Okanagan—ones that whisper through its lakes, its mountains, and its people. Writing *Guardian of the Lake* has been a celebration of history, mystery, and the ties that bind us to the land and to one another.

With deepest thanks,
Dr. Constance Santego

The Author

Dr. Constance Santego

Dr. Constance Santego is a celebrated author, educator, and holistic healer whose work seamlessly blends storytelling with themes of mystery, healing, and personal transformation. With a doctorate in Natural Medicine and decades of experience in the healing arts, Constance brings a unique depth to her writing, guiding readers on journeys of both heart and spirit.

Growing up in the Okanagan Valley, surrounded by its natural beauty and rich history, Constance developed a deep-rooted connection to the land she calls home. Her father's grandparents settled in Vernon in 1912, and her mother's family arrived in Kelowna in 1944, establishing generations of ties to the region. This heritage inspires Constance's novels, where the stunning landscapes, vibrant communities, and enduring legends of the Okanagan shine through every page.

In her latest work, *Guardian of the Lake*, Constance transports readers to Okanagan Lake's shimmering waters, mysterious depths, and rugged cedar shores. Through themes of legacy, cultural connection, and the courage to embrace the unknown, she invites readers to uncover the mysteries of the lake and the stories that bind us to the land.

When she's not writing, Constance enjoys life with her husband in Kelowna, where she finds inspiration in the quiet moments by the lake, exploring local history and fostering personal growth in those around her. Whether through her stories, teachings, or explorations, she remains dedicated to her mission: to craft narratives that heal, uplift, and connect us all.